WICKED

WICKED

The Pack of St. James

NOELLE MACK

BRAVA

KENSINGTON BOOKS

www.kensingtonbooks.com

BRAVA BOOKS are published by

Kensington Publishing Corp.
119 West 40th Street
New York, NY 10018

All Kensington titles, imprints, and distributed lines are available at special quantity discounts for bulk purchases for sales promotion, premiums, fund-raising, educational, or institutional use.

Special book excerpts or customized printings can also be created to fit specific needs. For details, write or phone the office of the Kensington Special Sales Manager: Attn.: Special Sales Department. Kensington Publishing Corp., 119 West 40th Street, New York, NY 10018. Phone: 1-800-221-2647.

Brava and the B logo are Reg. U.S. Pat. & TM Off.

ISBN-13: 978-0-7582-2280-0
ISBN-10: 0-7582-2280-7

First Printing: September 2009

10 9 8 7 6 5 4 3 2 1

Printed in the United States of America

Chapter 1

Light hems swirled over dancing slippers and polished boots stepped in measured time over the ballroom floor. Semyon Taruskin saw nothing else—he had to look down as he made his way through the crush to avoid the yearning gaze of a certain young lady who had pleaded with him just last night to ravish her, so in love was she.

He had refused her—gallantly, of course, telling her that she was too innocent and too sweet for him. But the truth of that statement had only aroused her more. He'd had to untwine her soft arms and unclasp the lovely hands that caressed whatever she could reach of him, before bidding her a soft adieu and beating a hasty retreat past the dozing aunt in the corner.

He straightened as he came in to the next room, a smaller chamber where male guests swilled punch from crystal cups and joshed each other in loud voices.

Semyon gave an inaudible sigh, hoping to find more interesting company.

Female, of course. Witty and pretty. There had to be one or

two in attendance. Without thinking overmuch about where he was going, he went down a narrow hall, staying behind a footman in livery. The fellow walked slowly, his arms laden with winter cloaks trimmed in voluptuous folds of fur, plainer mantuas, and fine shawls woven in designs of infinite complexity. The things he held shifted with each stride, trying to escape his grip, seeming oddly alive.

But then it had not been long, perhaps only seconds, since each cloak and shawl had warmed the woman who wore it. The thought was pleasant. Semyon caught a whiff of the delicate scent of perfume and powder that the feminine garments exuded. Following idly to see where they would go, he imagined the bare, silky shoulders that had been caressed by the luxurious heap of stuff in the footman's arms and smiled to himself.

At the end of the hall, the footman stopped outside a wall of shimmering fabric, its golden folds and swells illuminated from within and showing the silhouette of a woman.

No, it was not a wall, Semyon saw, but a double set of floor-to-ceiling curtains looped on a rod that were pinned closed by a most ingenious device—no, it was not a device but hands.

Semyon looked closer. Slender fingers with oval nails held the curtains together, fingers that undoubtedly belonged to the silhouette. When the footman announced his presence on the other side and his wish to be relieved of his burden, the hand let go of the brocade and pushed one of the curtains back.

The light from the candle sconces in the hall fell upon a woman of such surpassing beauty that Semyon almost gasped. A maidservant? Somehow that seemed unlikely. He drew back into the shadows. She did not seem to see him.

Her hair was pinned up in a delectable tangle of curls, glowing a flickery dark red in the candlelight. The shape of her body was clearly visible. With the inner light of the improvised chamber behind her, he could see her sensually small waist and the long, smoothly rounded thighs that brushed each other as she took a step forward to take the things from the footman.

Ah. He almost moaned aloud at that sight.

Were he by some fortunate trick of fate to become her lover, he would feel privileged indeed to lift her skirts and touch the inside of those fine thighs . . . he knew exactly how they would feel. The shoulders and bosom revealed by her diaphanous gown shone in the soft light. The lovely, immodest rest of her, no longer concealed, would be just as tempting, and the skin on the inside of her thighs like hot satin. It was far too easy to imagine his hand caressing her there.

Semyon pressed back against the wall, still watching as she exchanged a few words with the footman, who bent forward at the waist to tip the bundle of garments into her outstretched arm. One of the heavier cloaks escaped both of them in the transfer and slid to the floor, causing the footman to swear.

"Never mind, Jack. You must go back without delay. I am sure there are many more ladies waiting in the foyer."

"Then let them wait, Angelica."

So that was her name, Semyon thought. And how it suited her. In her plain gown of white with no adornment upon her neck or ears but the curling tendrils of her hair, she might well have passed for an angel in some low church.

Jack was about to disobey her request and pick up the cloak when a stern male voice called from the other end of the hall.

"That is Kittredge," she said in a quiet, cultured voice, "and it sounds as if he is in a swivet. You must go, Jack."

The footman scurried off, consigning all butlers to the

flames of Gehenna under his breath. The swiftness of his departure caused all the candles but one in the hall to sputter and go out.

Excellent. He might observe her a little longer in peace, Semyon thought, without disturbing or frightening her.

Angelica left the fallen cloak upon the floor and moved back into the curtained chamber, putting each of the others in some place where it might easily be found. She chose the back of a chair for the light shawls, hanging the mantuas on a rack brought there for that purpose, and tossing the most splendid of the fur-trimmed cloaks over a dressmaker's figure.

Then she went back for the fallen cloak, bending down to pick it up, her breasts nearly escaping the confines of her bodice. He longed to cup them. Just that would be enough, feeling the tender nipples in the very center of his palms and—

She was shaking out the cloak, sending a gust of air his way. It smelled sweetly of her or perhaps of the things she'd handled. He didn't know, but he didn't stop breathing it in avidly.

Her every motion made her soft flesh quiver slightly and Semyon felt his groin tighten. Absently, she brushed a few bits of lint from the cloak with her slender fingers and flicked them away. He grew impossibly stiff—ah, to be stroked *there* so softly and then flicked a bit by such feminine nails. He gritted his teeth.

She held up the cloak with both hands for a final inspection and turned to go back in to the curtained room.

He could not help himself. Semyon stepped forward, slipping his coat off and holding it in his arms and giving a discreet cough to warn her of his presence.

"Back so soon, Jack?" she murmured, putting the cloak she'd picked up over the one already on the dressmaker's figure.

"No," said Semyon.

She gave a start at the sound of his unfamiliar voice and regarded him with wide, wary eyes that he thought were green.

"Where did you come from?"

He nodded in the direction of the ballroom, nonplussed by the directness of her question. "I was dancing—it is quite warm—"

She seemed uninterested in his stammered explanation. "How long have you been standing there?"

"Not very long. I am sorry if I startled you, Miss—?" he paused, hoping she would tell him her last name. Her face seemed faintly familiar, but then he had been staring at her hungrily from the first second she'd opened the curtain.

"Miss Harrow." She seemed to take his respectful address for granted at first, then gave her head an infinitesimal shake as if she'd had second thoughts about that. It occurred to him that even if she was now a servant, she had not been born into that class. "Or if you like, just Angelica. That will do," she said in a composed voice.

"As you wish." Knowing her first name, another man might have attempted further liberties with her, but Semyon remained respectful—and suddenly very curious. Only a well-trusted maidservant would be given the task of seeing to expensive cloaks and furs at a grand ball, but there was nothing servile about her.

Her pride and breeding showed in the way she held herself. Not haughty but confident. And so beautiful that she would outshine all other women present tonight. She belonged on the dance floor in the arms of one adoring partner after another, not behind a curtain at the end of a hall. Semyon wondered how on earth he might speak to her where there was no chance of interruption by a returning footman or anyone else.

Not now, evidently . . . she was looking at him in a way

that did not invite him to talk to her. He felt unnerved by the steadiness of her regard.

"Ah yes—my coat. Here you are." He held out his coat. "As I said, it is rather warm in the ballroom."

She came closer and inclined her head in a gracious nod that effectively dismissed him as she took it from his hands, quite careful that there was no inadvertent contact. No doubt she was accustomed to wandering men propositioning her at parties just like this one or angling to touch her in some way and she probably hated it. He glanced in to the room as she went back in, noticing with chagrin that there were no other men's garments in sober black to be seen.

Everything else was embroidered, sequinned, furred, and patterned—all women's things. She must think him a fool for having come here at all.

He managed a smile and made the briefest of bows, turning around to go back until he heard her soft voice.

"Sir—"

"Yes?"

"I do not know your name." Her lips pressed tightly together as if she was trying not to laugh. "And if other men take it into their heads to do what you have done, then I might mix up your coat with someone else's." She reached for a small pencil and a piece of paper, placing it on a book for a hard surface to write upon and looking at him expectantly.

Semyon nodded, as if the matter was of grave importance. "I understand. If you like, I'll take it to wherever it is supposed to be—"

She shook her head and gave him a small smile. "No, that is not necessary. But I would like to know your name."

"Semyon Taruskin," he said. "At your service."

She wrote it down as if she knew how to spell it—or, indeed, knew him. Again that faint feeling of familiarity nagged at him, but he just could not place her.

With a swift gesture, she tucked the piece of paper in the pocket of his coat. "Enjoy the ball, sir," she said matter-of-factly, essentially dismissing him.

"I shall. And I expect my coat will not mind keeping company with so much feminine frippery."

She nodded, acknowledging his jest with only a nod.

He found himself envying the damned coat for the way she was holding it. Not too tightly. Absently stroking it with just a fingertip while she looked steadily into his face.

Her eyes were green, a springtime shade, but they held shadows. Of fear? Sadness? He could not begin to tell. A feeling of unreality stole over him, as if he had been spirited into this out-of-the-way chamber and not walked there on his own two feet, simply because he was following a footman going about an ordinary duty.

Of course, it was not by his own will that he had come here tonight at all, but his older brother Marko had dropped too many hints to ignore. Kyril, the oldest of the three Taruskins, would have insisted: the wolf-blooded Pack of St. James had to keep up public appearances while they handled other, private matters for the king—matters that required an equal measure of discretion and viciousness.

Semyon, the not very dutiful youngest of the three Taruskins, had given in, not knowing he would have to dodge the unwanted attentions of a romantic girl, or that his effort to do so would cause him to wander down a hall at random and find a veritable goddess behind a golden curtain.

A goddess who seemed to be losing patience with him at the moment.

"Thank you, Miss Harrow."

She lifted a very elegantly arched brow.

"Angelica, I mean." He turned away from her with an effort and strode back through the hallway, toward the distant music of a quadrille.

* * *

It was an hour later when he returned, as soon as he thought it was not too obvious an attempt to talk to her again.

He had glanced about for Jack, hoping the footman would not interrupt him with Angelica, and spotted him under the stairs, sipping from a flat brown bottle with Kittredge. No doubt it was or had been filled with whiskey. They were red in the face and laughing together.

The ball was in full swing, nearly a riot by any estimation. Puffed-up bucks were down to their waistcoats and shirts, essaying leaps and other embarrassing steps to ever-louder music, while the women looked on from behind fluttering fans. The crush of guests on the side was close to unbearable and the stench of too many people in too small a place revolted him.

No one would notice his departure and he wasn't leaving, really. If anyone saw him leave the floor where he'd taken an obligatory turn or two with the better dancers, they would assume he was swilling punch somewhere or vomiting off a convenient balcony.

The one person in attendance who'd looked much at him, meaning the amorous young lady with the longing gaze, had disappeared, along with her mama. As to what the girl saw in him, Semyon could guess. It was not thoughts of marriage that addled her brain, but rather his reputation as a lover. He could hardly be considered all that eligible, not with his Russian name and the mystery surrounding his clan, ensconced though they were in a house so near to St. James's Square.

Their mysterious comings and goings caused no end of whispers. As for the murders that Marko had solved a year ago—it had not helped that one of their number was among the guilty. And the bizarre affair of the tsar's missing objet d'art, the Serpent's Egg, had Kyril departing for the far north of Russia—well, even without those two things it was hard enough for a wolfman to hold his head up in London, let alone howl.

No, Semyon, the most English in manner of the three, had much preferred to blend in. Let sleeping wolves lie. No one had come around the Pack looking for trouble in some time and they liked it that way.

He headed down the hall again, where the sole candle was down to a nub in the sconce, flickering as if a wind were blowing through. Yet the air was more still than before. The fragrance of woman was stronger too, assaulting his sensitive nose and making him think of Angelica.

The gold curtain up ahead was still illuminated by the lantern within the space, glowing, drawing him near. There was no silhouette against it now—perhaps she was sitting down. Or perhaps she had left.

He walked the remaining distance to it, letting his boot heels strike firmly on the bare wood floor so that she would hear him coming. No one inside the curtain rose; no one spoke.

Semyon slid a hand between the panels and looked in. Angelica was there.

She was asleep on a pile of coats. There had been too many in the end, he supposed, as more and more guests arrived, and there was no place to put them all.

In her hand was a red rose and she clutched the stem, her fingers moving nervously. It was newly budded, tight and fresh, still with just a trace of sparkling dew on its furled petals.

It seemed to him that she held it to her lips. As if a lover had given it to her.

He felt a furious jealousy that surprised him, and then disgust. Had she let herself be taken against the wall by some man, standing up like a common strumpet, and then collapsed in sleepy lust? There was no divan or chaise in the chamber, let alone a bed. What maidservant would risk being sacked by lying with a man upon the clothes of her betters?

He reminded himself that she was most likely not a servant. Semyon studied her in silence for several moments, sniffing the air and thinking. He caught no smell of sexual congress, he could be sure of that much, but nothing else. Perhaps the rose had been given to her by a male guest as a gallant gesture and nothing more.

Gradually, as his jealousy eased, something else took its place.

Arousal.

Her pose reminded him of the paintings some gentlemen hung in their private rooms. The sort that usually featured a beautiful woman, perhaps a shepherdess with skin like porcelain, her glorious hair a-tumble and her gown half falling off, barefoot, asleep in the hay as a sturdy farm lad happened upon her, agog with surprised desire.

The sort of painting that a new wife consigned to a distant room or sent off to be sold in a London bric-a-brac shop. In the flesh, living and breathing, Angelica was in every particular the sort of woman that would worry an inexperienced young wife. An older one might be grateful in her way for the sort of respite she could provide.

Perhaps she had been a lady's maid, hired for her good breeding and taste, until some unfortunate event had consigned her to the lower depths of this household.

She had seemed too intelligent to have fallen for the wiles of a master bent on seduction. Certainly the owner of this grand pile of stone in Mayfair, who had danced with someone else's wife all evening, had a reputation for chasing his female servants, but what of it? So many gentlemen in London did. Had she been forced, then, by a thoughtless and selfish master, and demoted in rank by her long-suffering mistress?

Angelica gave an almost inaudible moan through her parted lips. On the lower one he saw—or thought he saw—a faint trace of the dew upon the rose.

He kneeled beside her. His hand hovered over the sweet curve of one thigh, longing to stroke it, but he drew it back.

Her breaths made her bosom rise and fall in her uneasy slumber and he could not help but look. Such tender flesh. The idea that she had ever been manhandled made him angry.

Invited to touch her in an instant fantasy, Semyon imagined her arching drowsily with pleasure as he caressed both breasts, releasing them from her bodice, then mounding and squeezing the malleable flesh to erotic heights so that the nipples—pink, erect nipples—jutted out.

He would feast upon them, suckling avidly, one hand caressing the low curve of her belly until he felt the tremors of deep feminine arousal begin.

And then—*ah, my sleeping angel*, he thought fondly, *you have no idea what I am thinking or that I watch you. Dream, dream as you lie there on all that fur and finery and I will put it in your mind too.*

He would take her hands and place them upon her bared breasts, telling her to continue his caresses while he watched and undid his breeches. Were she wanton enough, and he suspected she would be, her slender fingers would clasp her nipples and tug, then move to cup her breasts and squeeze them in a rhythm that both satisfied her and made her want more.

The thought made his cock spring powerfully upward, constrained by the soft, thin leather of his breeches, which remained buttoned. He did not dare touch the manifestation of his manhood or her, but let his fantasy take over until the sleeping woman before him shimmered in his mind, awakened and wanting him.

He would tell her to lift her skirts, slowly. As the white material was drawn up, and she showed her legs and her thighs, a dainty triangle of curls and a flash of her most intimate, succulent flesh.

He would waste no time in assisting her to fully spread her thighs and reveal the nether lips, neat and plump, to his hot gaze. She, of course, could not see herself in that way, but that did not matter. She would sigh with pleasure when his probing finger slid into her and lift her hips instinctively.

He would bring her a taste of herself, touching his slick finger to her mouth and asking that she lick it.

Then—he leaned upon one hand, looking ardently at the vision of unviolated beauty sleeping before him—his tongue would go where his finger had been. Lapping with just the tip, then thrusting as deeply as she would let him. Teasing the tiny bud that held the most intense pleasure for a lady. Overwhelmed by the sensation, craving more, she would bend her spread legs and clasp them behind the knees to give herself more freely.

An excellent reason for him to raise his head, then, and push her clasped legs gently back against her shoulders, telling her to hold them so that her bottom was lifted off the bed.

Then he would see all, from glistening curls to swollen bud to the flushed lips of her sex, and finally to the tiny puckered hole where a fingertip might stray and stimulate, if she wanted that. Her wanton display would call for further delights. Her plump buttocks he would fondle, perhaps a little roughly, as his tongue lavished her snug cunny with silky-wet strokes and soft penetration.

Completely his at that moment, her body lifted and held in his hands, her first orgasm for him would be an intense one, an experience to savor while he controlled his own bursting desire.

Ahhh. He bent his head and closed his eyes, still not actually touching her, wondering if the sleeping, fully clothed woman before him had experienced the compelling fantasy in slumber as he'd hoped. He let his lust ebb away.

Semyon could not bear to wake her. If he was caught with her, the gossip would be all over London in an instant. If she had come down in the world and he suspected as much, she might fall still lower, though he had done nothing but look at her.

His sensual reverie had taken no more than a few moments, but he was stiff all over as he got to his feet.

Angelica slept on.

His coat—where was it? He hoped she was not lying on it, but then he spotted it easily enough. It was still the only masculine article of clothing in the room and had been hung up with care by itself. He shrugged into it, thrusting his arms through the sleeves, glancing into the mirror to adjust the lapels and make sure his erection had gone down. Given the size of his member, something still showed, but that was de rigueur at a ball that went on into the wee hours. He had no doubt that the buttoned-back bulge in the front of his breeches would be grabbed at by more than one tipsy female as he left.

Angelica's warm breath had made the rose unfurl its petals somewhat and he could see its innermost center, drenched with the same dew that had moistened her lip. Semyon smiled sadly. He hated to leave her. But if fatigue and the tedium of seeing to the needs of so many others had claimed her so utterly, he had no right to wake her.

There was always tomorrow.

He would make inquiries and find out more about her—and her master and mistress and well. How she had come to this house, whether she had ever been "upon the town," in the polite phrase, ever married, been widowed, run off with a soldier—in short, everything.

From down the hall he heard the coarse but not unfriendly

voice of Jack. The footman was alternately singing in snatches and muttering to himself.

Semyon stepped outside of the curtain. "Miss Harrow has fallen asleep," he said to Jack.

"Miss Harrow? Do you call her that? Very kind you are, to treat her so respectful, when she is no more than an upstairs maid." The footman peered at him "Downstairs, now, of course." Then he looked at Angelica. "Now that will never do," he said, remembering who he was and where he was. "But the ladies as what wants their things might like them warmed, though." He winked at Semyon.

"I could not bring myself to wake her," Semyon said softly.

"Then I must." Jack tottered into the room and leaned over the sleeping woman, speaking to her in a loud whisper. "Cor—Angelica, wake up. What if the mistress sees you sprawled like this, hey? Wake up."

She stirred and pushed the footman away almost violently.

"Will she be all right?" Semyon asked.

"I am sure she will, sir," Jack said, returning his attention to the chore, though Semyon would not call it that, of awakening the slumbering beauty on the heap of cloaks. The footman looked up when he heard the clink of a masculine fingernail on a heavy coin, just in time to catch the guinea that Semyon tossed to him.

"Take good care of her," was all he said.

"That I will do. Good night, sir. And thankee." The footman looked down at Angelica like a fond but somewhat exasperated brother, and leaned over her again, shaking her by the shoulder. "Now do as I say, and wake up!"

Semyon left the way he had come, instinctively sure that Angelica was safe with Jack.

※　※　※

Not too long after that, he had reached the Pack's lair in St. James by a circuitous route that involved a stop at his club, where he was plied with strong spirits. He was feeling rather the worse for his indulgence and headed straight for the massive staircase leading up from the door, wanting nothing but the security and peace of his own chambers to sleep it off.

A soft hand on his arm forestalled him, and a gentle voice murmured an inquiry in Russian.

"Natalya," he sighed. "I am going to bed."

The young wife of their housemaster spoke in English, since he had. "I wanted only to give you a message, Semyon."

He looked down at the shining crown of braids interlaced with ribbons upon her head—inside this house, Natalya favored traditional Russian dress in all its colorful glory. Outside of it, her braids and bright embroidered tunics were hidden under hats and coachman's coats in winter.

"Yes?"

"A man came to the door inquiring after you in the middle of the evening. You were at the Congreves' ball—"

"You did not tell anyone where I had gone, I hope," he said severely. The Pack lived under rules of strict secrecy as to their whereabouts.

"Of course not, Semyon," she said with some heat. "Do you take me for stupid?"

Semyon shook his head, reminding himself of her rare courage and cleverness in defending the Pack. "No. Forgive me, Natalya. I am tired and have had too much to drink—" He broke off, realizing he had given her a reason to brew her bitter-tasting herbal remedy for such self-induced ailments.

He hated the stuff, and usually spat it out when she wasn't looking. Tonight, though, it seemed to him that she was done with her household tasks and perhaps eager to talk to someone. That he would do but he did hate being cosseted.

"Very well, Natalya," he said, not wanting to be rude to her. Her face broke into a wide, glowing smile and she dashed in to the kitchen to put the kettle on the hob.

He followed into her realm. The room was a mix of Russian coziness—it boasted an enormous tile stove upon the top of which a boy slept at night, though he was not there now— and up-to-date English conveniences, marvels of kitchen engineering. The hearth was carefully banked with ashes, but she stirred up the high pile of embers and tossed a few pieces of cut wood upon them. Flames blazed up quickly under the kettle's dented bottom.

She had just finished baking, evidently, and several dark loaves were cooling on a rack. Natalya peered in to the kettle, added a little more water to it, and took pinches of dried herbs from jars in a rack and put them in a teapot. She ground peppercorns in a little mill into its open top and last of all added little twisty dried things from an earthenware jug stoppered with a cork.

Semyon had no idea what the dried things were. Natalya's potions were best drunk with eyes closed and nose held. But they did work.

When the kettle sang, she poured the boiling water into the teapot and sniffed appreciatively. Semyon hid a grimace. "Let that steep," she said.

They chatted agreeably enough about who had been at the ball, finally coming around again to the forgotten subject of the man who had called when he was out.

"Did he leave a card, Natalya?" Semyon asked.

She shook her head, preoccupied with pouring out the medicinal brew into a large mug.

"Then what did he say?"

"Not much. Only that he hoped you would be in tomorrow. So that was the message."

"Nothing in writing, eh?"

"No. I gathered that he wanted to talk to you privately."

Semyon shrugged, unconcerned. "If he comes back, then I will, I suppose. I hope he is harmless." He yawned hugely, suddenly revealing the hidden fangs that were the mark of the Pack men as his curling tongue touched the top of his mouth.

Natalya pretended to be shocked. "Don't scare me like that, Semyon."

He smiled lazily. The effects of the liquor were beginning to wear off. "Sorry. Your dear husband Ivan is here to protect you, is he not?"

"Ivan is sound asleep. Can you not hear him snore?" She gestured vaguely in the direction of the bedroom allocated to the housemaster and his wife.

"No, and that is a good thing."

She laughed and pushed the disgusting-smelling mug to him. "Must I?" he groaned.

"Yes." She put her hands on her very womanly hips and looked at him squarely. "While I watch."

His lips quirked, thinking of how much he had enjoyed watching someone else under very different circumstances. Should he tell Natalya of the sleeping maidservant? He could embellish the story to amuse her—of course, he would leave out the salacious fantasy he'd indulged in. But he would make the most of his impression that Angelica Harrow was too well bred to be a housemaid and also that her eyes held a hidden sadness. A beautiful heroine with both those qualities sounded like the beginning of a fairy tale, and his recounting of their brief meeting would appeal to Natalya, who was sentimental when she was not fierce.

He began the story of Angelica, hoping to distract her, then took a sip, scowling. He wanted to gag. Miraculously, the brew stayed down.

"All of it," Natalya said.

"The potion or the story?"

"First drink that," she scolded him.

Semyon sighed and lifted the mug, holding his nose as he tossed the steaming contents into his mouth, swallowing it all in one go like a trencherman at an inn. He gasped when he set the mug on the table, wiping away the tears streaming from his eyes.

"Very good," she said, evidently pleased with him. "That's over with."

"I think you have poisoned me," he said weakly. "Send roses to my funeral, if you please."

"What color would you like?"

"Ah—red."

"Indeed not. Red roses are for lovers. No, a ghostly white spray of lilies would do for you, I should think."

"It is the middle of winter." He coughed against the sour tide rising in his throat. "Hothouse blooms are too costly. No, bury me plain, if you please." His idle jests did not quite take his mind off the red rose Angelica had been holding in her sleep. Natalya's innocent remark made him wonder again who had given it to her and why.

Natalya went to the loaves she'd baked and tore off a chunk. "Eat this," she said. "It will take the bad taste away."

He sank his teeth into it, relishing its warmth and dark, earthy flavor, an echo of the faraway homeland he barely knew. Ivan's wife was truly a treasure. He dusted the few crumbs from his hands, smiling at her again.

"Now," she said, settling herself on a stool. "You did not tell me enough about the ball."

"It seems to me that I have run through the entire guest list and made unkind comments about nearly all of them. What else would you like to know?"

"What the women wore, from first to last."

"I beg your pardon?"

Natalya glared at him. "The night is cold, so begin with their cloaks and furs and hats, and then go on to"—she dropped her voice to a sensual whisper—"what lay beneath."

"Oh, I see," he laughed. "Well, a gaggle of lady's maids divested the female guests of everything they wore on top before they went into the ballroom, and then a footman took it all away. The gowns were certainly very pretty, although I cannot remember specific details, Natalya."

"Then who was the prettiest woman there?" she asked eagerly. "I am sure you remember that."

He nodded, making her wait for it. "Her name was Angelica Harrow and she was not exactly at the ball."

"No? Then where was she?" She looked at him narrowly. "You are a master of seduction from what I know and not to be trusted."

"The footman brought her the cloaks and wraps to put away and guard until their owners would want them again."

"She was a maid?"

"I think she wanted to give that impression," Semyon said carefully. "But to my ear and eye, she was not bred to the task."

Natalya looked sad and sympathetic. "Alas. A ruined beauty, forced to slave for a pittance."

Her melodramatic turn of phrase made him smile a little. "I have no idea."

She tore off a chunk of bread for herself and chewed it absently. "And did you engage her in conversation?"

"I merely handed her my coat. But yes, we exchanged a few words."

Natalya nodded, thinking it over. "I thought you seemed different somehow when you came home."

"I was drunk."

She waved a hand. "Not that. Something else—you seemed

to be elsewhere, as if you were thinking of something or someone lovely. Not the sots at your club, certainly."

He acknowledged her remarkable intuition with a nod. "Well done, Natalya. Angelica was on my mind from that moment on tonight. I hope to find out more about her."

"And when you do, will you tell me everything?" she asked eagerly.

"If I think it is fit for your pretty ears, yes, most likely I will."

"I am a married woman now," she said indignantly. "You can tell me anything. You and I are the youngest among everyone in this gloomy house, so you must. Who else am I to talk to? Not old Levshin—his nose is always buried in his ledgers. And Antosha is forever scribbling. I believe he is writing a history of the Pack."

"For many reasons, it will never be published," Semyon said.

"In any case, only those two are around much, so you have to talk to me when I need to be amused."

"I will do my best," he laughed.

Natalya nodded, pulling off another chunk of fresh bread and adding jam to this one, as if she needed to be fortified for the next installment of gossip. "If this Angelica took your coat from you, she also gave it back," she said slyly. "So you spoke to her twice."

"Ah—not at our second meeting."

"Why not?"

"She had fallen asleep on the pile of furry things. Holding a rose."

Natalya sighed. "Poor thing. But someone admires her besides you, it seems."

Her sly remark hit home and Semyon knew she was aware of it. "Yes, well, that is neither here nor there," he said briskly.

"I found my coat myself and left our sleeping beauty to the footman."

"Will you see her again?" Natalya asked innocently.

Semyon wanted to make some equally sly response but found to his surprise that he did not have the heart to do so. He looked straight into Natalya's wide questioning eyes and said only one word.

"Yes."

Chapter 2

The same night...

Angelica awoke at last, but not where she had been. The curtain-draped room in the Congreve house, its walls and furnishings, the cloaks and furs given into her keeping, all of it had vanished in a swirl as utterly as if she had dreamed every detail.

Someone had come in to that place—a man—but who? She tried to think. Her mind was as blurry as her vision for some reason and she lifted her head to look around. She was lying on a bare wood floor, a cuff of cold iron around her ankle, a chain rattling from it to a bolt set into a beam in the wall. A feeble light came from a candle in the far corner, throwing circles of shadows upon the walls.

Who had brought her here? Not the handsome fellow with the foreign name who'd given her his coat. Not the footman Jack, who'd come and gone with armloads of women's things.

No. Someone different. An older man, someone she had

taken for a guest at the party, lost, as Semyon had seemed to be.

She clenched her fist and something sharp pricked her palm. Angelica lifted her hand and saw that she was holding a long-stemmed red rose. Then it came back to her in bits and pieces.

The older man had come in shortly after Simon—Semyon, she corrected herself. His name had been Semyon Taruskin and she had written it down on a piece of paper and put it in the pocket of his coat. Just in case some other man was to come by with a similar coat . . . she vaguely remembered telling him something like that.

She had spelled his name correctly and he'd seemed surprised but she had heard of him. Semyon had a rakish reputation that men envied, and women sighed over.

Several more layers of blur seemed to fall away as she held on to the rose, letting it prick her palm to aid her memory, not minding the thin trickle of blood from the first inadvertent wound or caring about the white dress that was tangled about her aching body.

Semyon's sudden appearance had startled her in the extreme. By the time the second man, the older one, came through the curtains, she had been less wary.

The rose in her hand . . . yes, he, the one who'd come after Semyon had been and gone, had given her that, a gesture that had puzzled her at the time as he'd said nothing about it. But she'd supposed he only meant her to hold it while he struggled out of his coat.

She had taken the rose politely, not inquiring as to whether it was to be presented to a sweetheart, or if he wanted its stem clipped and the bud fastened to his lapel, expecting him to tell her.

The older man had not said anything about it, just remained oddly quiet once he was out of his coat, holding that close to his body, as if he was waiting for her to do something. But what had he wanted? She still could not think clearly.

He had seemed reluctant to hand the coat to her, beginning to fiddle with the waistband of his breeches while she averted her eyes. She'd listened absently to the distant strains of music from the crowded ballroom, noticing how it and the dancers seemed to thunder in unison as the gathering became more and more boisterous.

He'd murmured a no when she'd finally asked if he needed a button sewn, praying that he would not. He just stood there, red in the face and sweating hard—his shirt was soaked with it and not clean to begin with.

In fact, he seemed to emanate foul smells from all over his body that she could not name, but decay was the strongest.

Angelica's nose had wrinkled and without thinking, she'd brought the rose she'd been holding to her face and smelled its sweet fragrance, liking its extraordinary freshness. Ignoring the unpleasant man, she'd touched a finger to its tightly furled petals, separating them and found that the heart of the rose was drenched with a curious, crystalline dew.

Longing to taste it, avoiding the man's gaze and his revolting appearance, she had ventured to sample the dew, putting a fingertip first in it and then to her lips . . . and . . . and . . . she had fallen, knocking over a small dressing table and the book she'd used to write upon that lay atop it.

Gasping, terrified, she'd pulled herself up by the lapels of Semyon's coat somehow, unable to stand. The masculine smell of it had given her a jolt of strength that soon dissolved—she had let go and fallen again, to her knees. The other man had laughed at her, his voice coarse, a mongrel's bark.

She'd tried to crawl away, escape the shadowy chamber and the strange intruder who had tricked her, holding on to the stem of the rose. It had seemed to grow thick in her hand, as thick as a young tree, and the bud had become as big as a human head.

Then her other hand had touched the fallen book and she tried to tear out a page, thinking wildly of leaving a note for someone to find. The man had kicked the book away before she could. Sobbing, she flung the rose away from herself, but the man forced it back into her hand, curling her limp fingers around it and squeezing painfully hard with his hand until its thorns pierced her skin.

She remembered no more after that.

Angelica looked with horror at the rose she still clutched. The innocent-seeming petals had held a potent and dangerous drug. She threw it into a corner and curled up in a ball when she heard footsteps approach.

Two people. Men, judging by the tread.

They stopped by her head. One bent down to test the chain attached to the cuff around her ankle, seeming to find it sound. Through her hair, she saw the heavy boots of the man doing that, boots with round, scuffed toes and a split sole on the left one that had been mended, not well. The other pair were far more elegant—they were riding boots that had cost a small fortune and were polished to a high shine. She could almost see her face in them—a tear-swollen, dirty face, she knew that, half covered with matted hair.

"Hello, Angelica," the owner of the boots said. "Pity, seeing you in such a disreputable state. You always prided yourself on your beauty, didn't you, my dear?"

The tip of one of the boots pressed into her cheek. Icy terror gripped her heart and her breath stopped in her lungs. She had known that voice all her life. Angelica looked up into the face of her stepbrother and fainted dead away at his feet.

* * *

Semyon was unable to sleep and left his bed, peeling off his nightshirt and dressing again, rather carelessly. But who would see or care in the dark streets of London as he roamed through them? He was thinking of Angelica all the while, slipping out and away from the Pack's house with such stealth that he awakened no one.

His preternaturally long strides took him first to a marketplace, already stirring in the hours before dawn. No one noticed him, occupied as they were with the business of setting up stalls and dickering with farmers. Dray horses stood shivering in their traces, stamping their massive hooves with dull clops, their heavy muscles exhausted with the effort of pulling wagonloads of winter vegetables over the rutted roads to the city. Semyon glanced without interest at turnips and mangel-wurzels piled higher than his head, the earth still clinging to their lumpy sides. Another cart held immense cabbages and small sprouts still on thick stems, green kale tucked in frilly bunches beside them.

Sturdy farm women, swaddled in wool shawls and skirts, clomped about in wooden shoes. They had come to sell pies and jellies and other dainties, upturning the baskets they'd carried everything in and arranging their wares on the flat bottoms.

An enterprising one of their number had a charcoal fire going in an odd contraption that only a tinker could have made and was doing a brisk business in tea and coffee, sold in mugs that the customers drank from and handed back.

He decided against having any. Her clientele had a raffish air, for the most part. The bristling mustaches and stained beards of the men and the cracked lips of the women seemed unhygienic, although they were enjoying the steaming brews.

He walked on, lifting his head. Ah yes. Swinging sides of beef rolled by on a wheeled rack pushed by a butcher's lad.

There was mutton too, unless he missed his guess, marbled with fat. But no lamb, not in winter. He could not help wanting to snag a hunk of raw meat. It was the wolf in him and he would not apologize for it.

If he did take a bit of meat . . . then what? He could not eat it raw. No, he would have to thrust a stick through it and roast it over a fire with the tramps and beggars that prowled the outer edge of the market.

They might accept him as one of their own, a highwayman in stolen clothes, he thought. Or they might knock him over the head and turn his pockets inside out.

Semyon chuckled and bought a meat pie to eat instead and devoured it in seconds, licking his fingertips inelegantly but with considerable pleasure.

Then he walked away from the market, tossing a shilling into a grimy palm that stretched out to him from a shadowy doorway, and nodding to a young kitchen maid and fat cook who bustled by with empty baskets over their arms, heading in.

After a time, he became aware that he was heading in the direction of the Congreve house. In another several minutes, he was there.

Wonder of wonders, the windows were still lit up. The last of the revelers were being helped into their sedan chairs and carriages, while Congreve himself and his much younger wife called their good-byes from the top of the imposing outside stairs.

When the final door was shut, he distinctly heard Penelope say, "Good riddance!"

Semyon smiled. His hand went to his throat to fix his cravat into a decent-looking knot, and he realized he had forgotten to wear one. He looked down. His shirt was half-in and half-out, and his unbuttoned coat flapped in the chilly wind off the Thames. At least his breeches were fastened properly.

Congreve murmured something placating to his wife that Semyon did not hear. But he looked up when she called to him suddenly.

"Mr. Taruskin! Whatever are you doing there? I thought you had gone long ago."

"I had, Mrs. Congreve." He ran a hand through his disheveled hair in a futile attempt at grooming. "But I could not sleep and decided, ah, to take a constitutional. I happened to walk down your street."

"A constitutional? At this hour? Have you gone mad? Come in and have a glass of sherry and whatever is left of the aspics and meats, and we will send you home at daybreak," she said.

Her husband chimed in. "Yes, do. We shan't sleep until the sun comes up. And you will catch your death of cold if you stand there upon the cobblestones."

Semyon hesitated. He had hoped to catch an early-rising scullery maid of theirs out and about, and quiz her discreetly about Angelica, not speak to the Congreves. But since the invitation had been issued, he would be a fool not to take advantage of it.

He bounded up the stairs, noting with dismay that there was a look of blatant lust in Penelope Congreve's beady eyes.

"You do look as if you just tumbled out of bed, Mr. Taruskin," she said admiringly, "with your tousled hair and that flush in your cheeks. And your clothes—dear me. Such romantic disarray. Have you left a lady sighing happily into her pillow, then?"

"No, Mrs. Congreve."

"You can tell me if you have. Who is she?" She swanned through the door, followed by her harrumphing husband, who seemed bored with her chatter.

Semyon hoped she would not flirt with him anymore. It was difficult as it was for him to ask the least little question about the pretty maid who had seen to the cloaks and coats. Penelope was too shrewd not to guess why.

"Come along, come along," Congreve said affably, turning to urge him inside when Semyon hesitated.

He nodded and joined the couple in their foyer where a maid barely able to stand on her feet stifled a yawn before they turned to her.

"Squiggs, take Mr. Taruskin's coat," Penelope said sharply to her, "and be quick about it."

"Oh—no. I would rather keep it on," Semyon said, "I won't stay long."

Squiggs, a stolid young woman, stepped back into position against the wall, her face a blank mask.

"Has the other girl gone, then?" he asked Mrs. Congreve.

"What other girl?" Penelope replied.

"The one named Angelica. I went down the wrong hall during the thick of things and met her by chance."

Penelope Congreve shrugged. "Do we have a servant by that name?" she asked her husband in an arch voice. He did not reply. "Congreve, I am talking to you."

He only grunted, too old and wise to take her bait.

The true nature of a marriage was fully revealed in the weary hours after a party, Semyon thought. Mr. Congreve might be guilty of indiscretions too numerous to name, but Semyon suspected that his cold-eyed wife strayed too. He hardly cared and it was too late to take back his inquiry. But he hated to think of old Congreve even trying to touch Angelica.

He would take her away from here, he decided suddenly. It would not be difficult to persuade her as soon as he could find her and talk to her.

If she wished to go, he reminded himself dutifully.

Bah. He had a feeling she would fling herself into his arms and beg to be rescued.

Once she was safely by his side, he would figure out what to do with her. Semyon had never been one for thinking further ahead than a day or two, a privilege of being the last-born of his brothers. They did his thinking for him and he ignored their good advice. He was as wild as he wanted to be.

"Her last name was Harrow, I believe. Or something like that." Semyon strove to keep his tone conversational, as if he didn't care in the least what had happened to a mere maid.

"Oh, her." Penelope shot a look of disgust at her husband, who appeared not to notice it. "Of course. Angelica. How could I forget *her* first name? Silly me." She favored Congreve with a thin smile. "We were giving Harrow one last chance with the coats tonight, weren't we, my dear?"

"I see." Semyon Taruskin waited for her to say more.

"He"—she went on, indicating her husband with a wagging finger—"hired her on a friend's recommendation—his friend, not mine—as a lady's maid for me. Sight unseen. Most unwise. I never quite trusted her and she seemed to think she was too good for the job, so it seemed best to take her down a peg. Mr. Congreve had to agree, as I vowed to make his existence a living hell if he did not. I always get my way."

On and on she prattled, leading both men into the library and heading for a decanter and set of small glasses. In other rooms of the vast house, he could hear servants putting things to rights and clearing away the debris of the party, and one occasionally passed through where they were, looking nervously at Mrs. Congreve first.

She handed round the filled glasses herself, sipping hers daintily but fast and refilling it several times as the conversation between the two men ebbed and flowed. Semyon was listening with only half an ear, hoping to catch a glimpse of Angelica or hear her soft voice over the hubbub. After a time, he made some excuse to leave, and bent over Penelope's outstretched hand in a pantomime of a gallant kiss, not about to touch his lips to her papery skin. Fortunately, she was quite drunk and did not seem to care what he did.

Semyon straightened. Mr. Congreve, he realized, had slumped in his chair, suddenly overcome by sleep in the manner of an aging man who had had too much sherry and stayed up too late.

As Semyon watched, the older man's mouth fell open and his tongue lolled within the pale pink cavern as he snored juicily.

"You see what I must contend with." Penelope dashed away a tear.

Semyon had no doubt that she felt infinitely sorry for herself and with some reason. But he was no closer to finding his goddess and could not very well prowl the house looking for her.

"Yes. I daresay he is tired. As we all are. Mrs. Congreve, I must go," he said firmly.

"Are you sure?" she asked in a tiny voice.

"Quite sure." He disentangled himself from the surprisingly strong grip of her hand on his arm and offered her a pillow instead. With a prodigious yawn that revealed every one of her neat, small teeth, Penelope flung herself into it, looking up at him coquettishly.

Semyon hastily withdrew, leaving the Congreves to each other and shutting the door to the library behind him.

He headed for the front door, glad he'd worn no hat that he might have forgotten in his haste to leave. Glancing into the rooms being set to rights, he looked around one last time for Angelica and spotted Jack instead.

The footman, whose livery had been replaced by work clothes to help the others move the ballroom furniture back to where it had been, gave him a worried frown and took him aside.

"Sir—may I talk to you?"

Semyon knew instantly that the other man's concern was for Angelica.

"Yes, of course." He let himself be led into an alcove where they would not be heard or seen should a busy servant pass by. "What is it?"

"Our Miss Harrow is gone, sir. I could not wake her after you left and when I went back an hour later, she was not there at all."

"What? Have you looked elsewhere in the house?" He controlled his tone and suppressed his instinctive fear for the beautiful woman he'd desired so much. Had some other man happened upon her as she lay in slumber?

"Of course or I would not have come to you," Jack replied. "She is not in her chamber under the eaves and none of the other women have seen her for some time. One said that the mistress was fuming because Angelica was not there to hand back the coats. It was a mad scramble, I hear—"

"Never mind that, man. Do you think Angelica was sacked and left because of that?"

"No. Her belongings are just as they were in her chamber, nothing taken. Only she is gone. And I put your very question to several of the servants. Someone would've heard something. Mrs. Congreve is a great one for making scenes and screaming. Her husband cannot control her and she does as she pleases."

"Hmph. I daresay she cannot control him," Semyon muttered.

The footman only shrugged, as if he had no particular concern for the Congreves. "Those two would not care if Angelica vanished forever. Something about it does not seem right to me, but I cannot say why. It is not like her—she was always kind to others and she would have left word with a sympathetic soul or told me had she decided to run away."

"So. It seems that no one would blame her if she did, am I right?" Semyon asked.

"The higher you go, the worse it can get in this unhappy house," the footman said soberly. "I was thinking that as Mrs. Congreve's maid, she might know more than the rest of us. But she never said. Things go on here behind closed doors that no one but the master and mistress can open."

"I see. That does not bode well."

Jack hung his head as if saying the briefest of prayers, then looked up. "You told me to take care of her, and I tried to, sir. And I would have done, gold guinea or no—"

Semyon's every hair stood on end. He was just as guilty, if anyone was. He too had left her where she lay, asleep and vulnerable. "Good God, man, where could she have gone? Who are her friends? Where is her family?"

"I don't know. None of us knew much about her. It is like that in London, sir—"

"Yes, yes, of course. Let us think only of this evening at the moment. What happened, exactly, after I left you two alone?"

"'She would not wake and I could not stay with her, not when mistress was shrieking for me. You must have left the house before that or you would have heard her too."

"Most likely I had, yes." His mind raced, considering various possibilities. "Jack, can you take me to the room where the cloaks were? Will we be noticed?"

The footman hesitated. "Where is the mistress? She will threaten to have me whipped from pillar to post. Her and Mr. Congreve fought over Angelica."

"Asleep on a pillow in the library after several glasses of sherry. Mr. Congreve is snoring in a chair beside her."

Jack nodded, as if that were something he'd seen many a time before. "Come with me then."

"It is the most logical place to start," Semyon said, low urgency in his voice.

In a little while, going this way and that, they came to the part of the house where the narrow hall and the curtained chamber were. On the way there they caught a glimpse of Kittredge heading upstairs with Mrs. Congreve, a limp burden in his arms, feigning sleep.

None of the servants seemed to notice it, or care that Jack was escorting a guest through the house.

They hurried down the hall. Even from the end of it Semyon could see that the curtains had been carelessly swept to one side, as if someone had departed from inside in haste.

The cloaks and furs and mantuas were all gone and the room had the appearance of being ransacked. It was difficult to tell the difference between the aftermath of a large party, though, when servants who were tired or drunk or both would scramble to retrieve milady's things. The few chairs leaned against the wall but one had been knocked over. The dressmaker's figure stood upright, a mute witness to what had happened here.

"I left her on that pile where she was, still a-sleeping," Jack said. "It was much later when I came back and that was to break up a fight between two lady's maids. Scratching and clawing they were, but Angelica was nowhere to be seen."

"Did you not search the house?"

Jack shook his head. "I was wanted elsewhere."

"There is a bad smell in the room," Semyon declared. "Of decay and worse."

Jack took a cursory sniff or two. "It smells the same to me, sir. But it has not been aired out. The high and mighty stink like anyone else, of course, and so do their clothes. Especially after a long night."

Semyon willed his wolf-sight into his eyes, turning his face away from Jack so that the servant would not see his pupils change to glowing gold. He strode to the wall, where he had discerned faint, long scratches.

Yes. He caught her smell underneath the lingering odor of decay, the cause of which he could not guess. As Jack had pointed out, many people had come and gone in this small space tonight.

He looked intently at the wall. The scratches had been made by fine fingernails, feminine ones, and it was clear to him that she had made them. Perhaps clawing at the wall, sliding down it after falling against it. Had she tripped over the pile when she had arisen at last? He had to consider the possibility that nothing of consequence had happened to her, that she had merely decamped, especially considering the antipathy between her and her mistress.

The possibility that she had gone off with an unknown lover—the matter of the rose in her hand still troubled him—was not something he wanted to think about.

The side of his boot touched against something hard. Semyon looked down.

He recognized the book she had used to write his name upon the slip of paper she'd put in his pocket. He bent down to pick it up and opened it.

A few pages had been torn and recently. A few fine threads of linen trailed from the jagged edge of the torn pages. He put it to his nose, catching the unmistakable scent of fear. Her hands had been sweating, her body exuding a nameless terror that only he could sense.

To Jack, to anyone, what he held was only a book. Semyon quickly riffled through the other pages to see if anything had been written in it in desperate haste—no. There was nothing.

The book was small enough to slide into his pocket and he did so, touching the slip of paper he had not thought of **until** now, the one with his name on it.

Hearing a noise of someone dashing about not far away, Jack had gone into the hall just outside. Semyon brought the slip of paper to his nose, smelling it for comparison.

The feminine hand that had touched it had left a trace of scent as well, but there was nothing at all fearful in it.

No, it was pure and sweet. He knew that seeing him had been a pleasant experience for her from that alone, and he studied the graceful handwriting. Just his name, written with care in pencil. He sensed that she had liked writing it and hope sprang high in his heart.

So little to go on. So much to be found out. Wherever she was in the teeming city, he would find her. And he would deal savagely with anyone who hurt her.

Semyon put the slip of paper back in his pocket with the book and joined Jack in the hallway.

"There is nothing here," he said with finality.

Chapter 3

Angelica struggled to open her eyes, knowing only that her cheek was pressed against something that scratched like wool. She lifted herself up on one elbow and looked warily around her. She had been dumped on a carpet in a different room and there were no boots, rough or polished, near her face.

Waiting for she knew not what, she held her breath and listened for the faint sound of someone else's breathing. There was nothing, but other sounds outside filled her ears.

She knew was still in London—she could hear the raw-voiced cries of street sellers and a hack driver clattering by, roaring at his horse in foul language that was nonetheless English.

Still, she could be anywhere. Good neighborhoods could be right next to rough ones like as not. Angelica was not about to dash to the window and scream for help when she was not even sure that she was alone in the room.

She seemed to be on one side of a high bed that boasted a mahogany frame with posts carved in spirals and a canopy in draped silk that would have been the pride of a Parisian demi-mondaine.

She was near the windows of the room, away from the door or doors that she could not see. She looked up and around herself again taking in every detail of the expensive but somehow tawdry furnishings. Affixed to the tasseled corners of the canopy were tiny cupids, swarming thickly as mosquitoes.

The louche décor was luxurious and sensual but the bizarre contrast to the austere chamber where she had first been imprisoned made her uneasy. She stayed where she was, convinced by now that she was alone in the room.

For now.

Knowing her stepbrother, he had brought her to a pretty prison for a reason that was bound to be ugly. Victor Broadnax was capable of ingenious and elaborate cruelty.

What he was planning—what he might do next—made her shudder and she forced her fears aside. Then she thought suddenly of the iron cuff around her ankle and curled over to feel for it. That too was gone. She rubbed the sore marks that gave evidence of it having been there at all, feeling as if she were moving through a waking dream.

Angelica moved closer to the bed and raised her head, venturing a look over the puffy coverlet. She saw no one but located the door, telling herself that it was undoubtedly locked.

Her only ways out were it or the windows. The angle of the sunlight streaming in and the distant quality of voices she'd heard from the street told her that she was probably on a high floor. She lifted herself up noiselessly by gripping one of the bedposts and took a few stealthy steps to the nearest window.

There was no betraying creak of floorboards underneath the carpet she'd lain on. Well and good.

Angelica stood to one side of the window's sheer curtains,

looking down at the iron railing that completely surrounded the narrow area between the house and the street.

A burly man stood there, thick-fingered hands clasped behind his back, wearing a heavy coat with an upturned collar and a nondescript hat. Passersby glanced into his face, which she could not see, and hurried past him.

So this side of the house was guarded. No doubt the back was too. She looked up and down the street below, not recognizing it at all. But then she had not been long in London.

The houses seemed new but they had a raw look, as if they had sprung ready-built from a former field on the outskirts of London. They were jammed together with no alleys or cuts in between, which would make an escape difficult to hide. She could not slip away unnoticed when she still wore the same plain white gown that had done for the hot little room with the cloaks. Not when she was . . . Angelica looked down . . . barefoot.

She heard heavy footsteps approach and pause. It seemed to her that were there were two sets, walking in almost perfect synchrony, but she was not sure. Then she heard the tiny grind of metal on metal, and realized that a key was turning in the lock. After another second it was withdrawn and the doorknob turned in the same stealthy way.

Angelica shrank back into the curtains, knowing that their gossamer folds would not hide her. But if worse came to worse, she could smash the window and jump—she glanced down again.

She was three storeys above the street, by her guess. She would be badly hurt, perhaps impaled on the railing. The guard below would carry her broken body swiftly away and someone else would pay handsomely for the silence of inadvertent witnesses.

The slowly turning doorknob completed its revolution and the door opened a crack. A plainly shod foot thrust through at the bottom and a woman came through with a tray. She didn't seem to see Angelica, didn't look around, just went straight to a table where she deposited the tray in her hands. She said nothing.

The woman turned and went back out, closing the door with a click. Her heavy footsteps retreated and eventually there was silence. Angelica breathed again. It occurred to her that she hadn't heard the doorknob turn again or the key and lock, and she wondered why.

It had to be a trap.

She could not open the door and run down the stairs. It could not be that simple.

Then, breaking the silence, the doorknob turned again and the door was locked once more. Someone on the other side—she had heard a second set of footsteps—withdrew the key.

Angelica wanted to shriek, to beg for her freedom, batter her way out—anything other than this sinister game of cat-and-mouse.

All she could do was listen very carefully. Her captor's footsteps echoed as he went away, sounding as correct as the polished boots he wore.

She looked again at the tray and the covered salvers on it. So Victor wanted her to eat. She remembered the crystalline poison in the rose and felt a wave of nausea. Weak as she was, she would not eat.

Angelica paced about the room, her thoughts in a tangle of fear and useless resolve. Until Victor decided to talk to her, she was his prisoner.

She sat down on the whorish bed and burst into tears.

Some hours later, when the sunlight was swallowed by the gathering blue of dusk, she found water in an ewer standing in a matching basin. Lifting the ewer, she splashed a few drops on her arm, testing it too for poison. Her skin did not sting or peel off. It seemed to be only water. She soaked a cloth in it and scrubbed at her face, then combed her hair.

She knew that Victor would come to her in due time—he preferred the night as a rule. Angelica wondered how he was connected to this house and whether he owned it. His recent inheritance would have been more than enough.

If he lived here, the room she was in held no trace of him and seemed entirely feminine.

Quietly as she could, she looked on shelves and opened and closed drawers, finding nothing of note. It seemed the sort of room that was used for assignations, with every sensual comfort but nothing of permanence about it.

Hungry and unbearably thirsty—she would not drink of the water in the ewer—she sat in an armchair and thought of when she had seen him last.

Victor had been dashing in his way, the younger image of his oafish father, her stepfather. Late and unlamented, Samuel Broadnax, who called himself a gentleman and was nothing of the kind, had been stricken with a fatal fever and died two days after her mother.

Try as she might, Angelica could not summon up any tenderness for that lady, who had wanted nothing to do with her from the very day of her birth, handing her over to a string of nursery maids and governesses.

They were all disagreeable and severe women to begin with and none had ever shown her the least kindness, per her mother's command. Of that Angelica had no doubt, having found written instructions to each of them in her mother's own handwriting.

The least infraction earned her a vicious birching on her bare legs well into her teens, a punishment that she, too cowed to think of escape, simply endured after a lifetime of intimidation and petty cruelty.

The revelation that her slightly older stepbrother had enjoyed watching the sessions shocked her greatly. She had never known at the time that he was there.

She had come to understand, from the only sympathetic servant in the household, that young master Victor got his way through bribery and mutually satisfying exercises in perversity with the woman who administered her beatings and lessons in geography with such vigor.

Still, the geography had come in handy—Angelica could not have found her way about London at all without her study of Roche's map of it when she finally did escape from her stepfather's country house.

With a small sack of money and only the clothes on her back, she had survived, hired out through a servant's agency as a lady's maid owing to her good looks and breeding.

The Congreves had been the last of three such assignments, and eluding Mr. Congreve's moist grasp had proved impossible. Angelica had loathed his wife, and longed to leave, knowing on the night she was left to handle the cloaks and furs that it might be her last.

Until Semyon Taruskin has come in to bring his coat to the wrong place, she had thought only of walking the streets as she had done.

He had been kind. Even courteous. She was not accustomed to either. When he'd told her his name, she had remembered it from the endless flow of gossip among the female servants in the Congreves' house.

Besides that, it had seemed to her that she had seen him somewhere before and perhaps she had in her rambles. The parks of London were a respite for her and she wandered into them on the rare occasions when she had a half-day to herself.

She was sure he rode and often. Her downcast eyes had not missed the strong muscles of his thighs, nor the strength of his calves. And he had the erect posture of an experienced horseman, from the top of his tousled dark head through his broad-shouldered back and long legs.

He'd seemed every inch the gentleman to her. If he lived near or on a fine square by the parks that the ton frequented to see and be seen in, then perhaps he had noticed her and she had smiled back . . .

Angelica strained to breathe through the sad tightness in her throat and forced all thoughts of her brief encounter with Semyon Taruskin away.

She would have to save herself somehow. No one was riding to her rescue.

Tears filled her eyes and rolled down her face, hot as her own blood. She didn't have the strength to dash them away. As the last glimmering of day faded from the sky outside the windows, she fell into a troubled sleep in the armchair.

An aching in her legs made her stir and slowly open her eyes—that, and the honeyed smell of beeswax. A man stood with his back to her, touching a lit candle to each wick of the tapers in a tall candelabra.

She recognized him and tried to get up without making a sound, but her stiffness from sleeping in a chair kept her trapped for the moment. So Victor had come in while she was as good as unconscious. She had no doubt he had looked through the keyhole first—she remembered him doing that at the country house, so often that she stuffed a tattered handkerchief into the keyhole when she disrobed or dressed.

"Did I awaken you, Angelica?" he asked without turning around, intent on his task.

She wanted to grab the candelabra, thrust the burning candles into his face, and run for her life. She half-rose, steadying herself on the arms of the chair, but her legs wobbled.

He turned around to face her and folded his arms across his chest. He seemed to her to have filled out, no longer a young buck of slight build, but a powerful, fully grown man.

The evil that drove him had grown in strength as well. She could see it in his eyes.

"It seems that I did. You can sit down. I will bring you the tray. You haven't eaten a bite."

"And I will not. Take it away."

His expression hardened. "Do not give me orders, my dear sister."

"I am not your sister!"

He only shrugged. "The law would have it so and who am I to argue with the law?"

Angelica was standing fully on her feet, feeling the blood flow again in her legs. Still, she doubted she could push past him, let alone escape.

"What do you want with me?" she asked desperately. "It was you I ran from, after you—you tried to touch me."

"So you did."

"You let me go then," she said in a pleading voice. "You cannot keep me prisoner in this house, Victor!"

"Are you a prisoner?" he inquired in a maddeningly calm tone.

She shook a fist at him, a futile gesture, for it only made him laugh. "You drugged me and kidnapped me or had someone do it—that man out there, was it? And I woke up shackled to a wall—where was that room? In this house or another?"

"So many questions," he reproved her. "I don't know where to begin."

She took a step forward and her skirts swung as she did. He glanced down, making her shrink back as if he had hit her.

"You are not shackled now," he said pointedly. "I don't do things like that to women, unless it is a game they like to play. Some do, you know. Guard and prisoner. Crime and punishment."

Angelica flushed with shame. "You thought such things

were games. You and that filthy little bitch who did her best to hurt me."

"Miss Hopkins was hired to correct your wayward nature, Angelica. Dear Nancy. She taught me much."

"She let you watch!"

Victor smirked. "Indeed she did. And it was not only you who was birched. At least you were permitted to keep your skirts down and receive your strokes only upon your legs. Things were rather different for the housemaids, you know. A well-run household cannot tolerate impertinence from the staff. I helped her with those sessions. And it was my very great pleasure to do so."

Angelica spat full in his face. Victor wiped away the few drops she had worked up from her dry mouth and took two steps toward her, holding her by the throat with one large hand and rubbing her spittle into her face with the other.

"Do not ever do that again," he growled. "You must show me respect at all times from now on."

She struggled to breathe, pulling at his hand. He kept it where it was, but loosened his grip fractionally.

"Wh-why d-don't you just kill me?" she gasped. "I will not be b-broken by you again—never!"

He let her go and pushed her back into the chair. Angelica fell into it like a rag doll cast aside by a petulant child.

"You are a valuable commodity, Angelica," he said after studying her for some moments. "And I am now a man of business."

"You are a dirty bastard and nothing more!"

He sighed and began to pace the room. "I should not have taken you by the neck. Your remarkable beauty must remain unmarred. You will fetch a higher price that way. Are you still a virgin, Angelica?"

"What?" The depth of his depravity was revealed in his last question. Truly, she would rather die if she could not escape!

"I could have the ox outside control you here and now. My bawd knows how to check, you know." He snapped his fingers. "Shall I do that?"

"No!" Her thoughts raced as she figured out the nature of his business. "Is that why you had me kidnapped? Why me? There are—there are thousands of women in London who would willingly sell themselves!"

He nodded sagely and stopped his pacing. "But it is the struggle that some customers desire—the unwillingness of the truly pure excites them, you see—I thought of you the first time I was asked to procure such a one."

"For shame, Victor!"

"Shame?" He grinned. "I don't know the meaning of the word. You will have to explain it to me. I believe Miss Hopkins instructed you in that humbling emotion often enough."

She fell silent, appalled and afraid. Yet she felt a flicker of hope. Nothing more. If he wanted to sell her unmarred, then she had a chance, however slender.

"How long has it been since you ran away into the night?" he mused. "Two years? Three? I thought I might find you when I came down to London but only once did I catch a glimpse. You were riding in a carriage by a lady, dressed in her second best as far as I could tell. I assumed you had gone into service as a maid."

Angelica let him talk.

"After all, you had no references and no sensible family would entrust their precious brats to an unknown girl who called herself a governess." He cast an assessing look at her. "And you are too proud to whore. I knew that."

She drew herself up unthinkingly.

"So that left working in a shop, which I did not think you would do. Too public. Or becoming a lady's maid. I was right, wasn't I?"

His expression was unbearably smug. She did not reply.

"But finding you was a problem, and of course I was establishing my business and had many other things to do. As you just said, there are many women in London who are willing to sell themselves. But my enterprise was specialized."

Shut up. She wanted to scream it a thousand times. She wanted to choke him, squeeze the foul life from his body and consign his soul to hell, but the thought of his far superior strength, to say nothing of his underlings in this house, put paid to that wild idea.

"It did also occur to me that you might become the mistress of a wealthy man, perhaps even the wife of one who didn't care to ask questions," he continued. "I see that didn't happen."

She shook her head, not that she was entirely surprised by his obsessive pursuit of her in the intervening years. "How did you find out that I worked for the Congreves?"

"The old man and I belong to the same club. He was in his cups, boasting of his conquests from a list he had in his hand. He happened to describe a young beauty, a new maid he'd hired for his wife and I thought it might be you. Then I looked at the list and I saw your name, plain as day. Angelica Harrow. He'd put a star by it."

"Why?"

"He explained that it meant you were next."

"I dodged him," she said flatly. "His wife had her suspicions, but she was entirely wrong."

"I see," Victor said cheerfully. "I do like the forthright way you say that. It sounds as if you are done pretending to be outraged."

He looked at her through narrowed eyes and it began to dawn on Angelica that she would do well to play along for the time being.

"You must know by now how the world works. Women

do not choose their destinies unless luck is on their side and it is not on yours. What do you think? Shall we come to some sort of agreement concerning your, ah, employment?"

She hesitated, unable to formulate a plausible lie in time.

"You don't want to be a maid or a draggletail, do you? My man found no money on you when he rolled you in burlap and took you out the back way of that huge house. Going downhill is all too easy for a woman with no family." He smirked again, more widely this time. "Am I not right, Angelica?"

She nodded and sank upon the bed, twisting her hands until they hurt, not looking at Victor, not seeing anything in her pain.

Chapter 4

Semyon hurried along, heading back to the house of the Pack, wondering if he should tell his kinsmen there of his concern for the missing woman. He decided against it.

The older members of the clan would advise him of the necessity for prudence and discretion as they always did. Some of the younger ones might mock his chivalry on behalf of a housemaid and he would have to fight them to preserve his standing.

As for his blood brothers, Kyril was far away and Marko—the middle Taruskin— was not likely to be interested in the complications of Semyon's love affairs. Natalya would be, especially since she'd heard the beginnings of the story. But she would never leave him alone until she knew whether it had a happy ending or, Great Wolf forbid, a sad one.

Where had Angelica Harrow gone? Why did he care so much?

He was not in love. Far from it. A woman—admittedly a very beautiful woman he had been powerfully attracted to, as if by an instinctive bond—had disappeared. There was no blood in the room where he had met her, no verifiable signs of a struggle outside of the marks of her fingernails in the plaster, a clue, perhaps, but one that could be interpreted in several ways. She might very well come back, heedless of the concern of her fellow servants and caring nothing for Semyon at all.

He really knew nothing about her, he mused, and what was more, had no idea where to begin. The wind grew stronger and he flipped up his coat collar, holding his chin down to keep his bare throat warm. Then he thrust his hands into his pockets and touched the slip of paper she had written on.

The fine hair on the back of his neck rose up and tingled as he did. A sure sign that his wolf nature had sensed some trace of her.

If she had walked from the Congreve house as he was now doing, his supernatural instincts might be following a trail that was not scent but an emanation. He tried to shut out what little activity there was on the street and listen completely to them.

She had come this way. He listened more deeply to his ten senses. Mortals had five. The Pack, descended from the mingled blood of great wolves and ancient heroes of the steppe, were doubly blessed. Along with sight, hearing, touch, taste, and smell they could boast of five more—though they never did boast—magnetism, memory that was centuries old and a sense of time that was older still, the ability to distinguish between falsehood and the truth, what was poison and what was pure, and the unerring recognition of true love.

So, he thought, leaning into the wind, he was safe enough when it came to the last.

Angelica. Her name seemed to hang in the cold air he moved through so swiftly. Startled, he realized that his wolf traits were coming to the fore as the sense of her grew stronger. His fingers pressed together in his pockets, becoming furred paws with long, thick nails. A ruff of fur prickled uncomfortably under his shirt, the longer guard hairs piercing the linen of it and then the silk of his waistcoat until they too were blunted by the much thicker material of his coat.

Damnation. He itched.

He could feel stubble growing quickly on his muzzle—chin, he told himself. Well, that was nothing strange upon the face of a man who gave every appearance of heading home to sleep off the effects of a party. He smiled at another maidservant who was coming from the market, noting that she glanced at the dark shadow on his jaw with barely hidden approval.

Women did like a bit of stubble and that was that. As for his paws—hands, he told himself—he would keep those in his pockets.

Semyon stopped at the corner, not knowing which way to turn. The instinctive response growing ever stronger directed him to the left, in the opposite direction from St. James's Square, his original destination. He looked down the street that led, as far as he knew, to what had recently been a field at its farthest end, swallowed up by the relentless growth of London and developed by building speculators.

The winter wind seemed to be coming from that direction and it was stronger than ever. There was nothing for it. He squared his shoulders and walked for two more miles.

Standing where the street abruptly ended, he glanced around, seeing a row of new town houses and a shabby old tavern, the sort that never closed. He could not knock on doors at the moment because he did not know the trick of willing paws to become hands again. It happened when it happened.

But if he found a quiet corner in the tavern, he could sip at a mug of ale without using either. A longish tongue helped with that. He pushed through the doors, glad to see the place filled with men, talking loudly and singing. He headed straight for the inglenook, where no one was, and sat down in front of a puny but comforting fire.

A wench came over and nodded when he ordered two tall mugs of the best ale, returning with them in both hands, yeasty foam slopping over the edge. He thanked her and she picked up the sovereign he'd set out before she came back, giving him a wink for his generosity.

He slouched down a bit more so no one could see him and licked at the foam, then lapped up the ale, getting halfway through both mugs.

Semyon sat back, satisfied.

"Done, are you?" The wench had returned. "Want another?"

"No."

She nodded, not put off by his bluntness. It was a working-man's tavern and finesse would have been out of place. He'd already given himself away a little with his handsome tip, but he reasoned she would not brag of that and risk losing it. Semyon rose and went to the bar to sit at the end of a row of bricklayers, judging by their immense shoulders and massive arms. The rough men quaffed ale and devoured slabs of bread and cheese, stuffing chunks into their mouths and chewing heartily.

"Lots of work for you lads, I see." He nodded toward the door and they seemed to understand that he was referring to the new houses on the street outside.

The bricklayer next to him shoved another. "Aye. We must eat and drink hearty-like to keep up."

"Are they sold?" Semyon asked.

"Aye. Most. A gentleman 'as moved in to one already. The rest are empty yet. But the street sellers are sleepin' in some these cold nights."

"Poor bastards'll be tossed out on their arses soon enough," said a stout fellow. "Pity. Like walking shops, they are, selling everyfink, and enough of us laborers about for them to profit. Shout like madmen all day, they do."

Grunted assents went down the row as the bricklayers finished their meal.

"So no one lives here then?" Semyon asked, hoping he would not be asked why he wanted to know.

"Nowt but the gentleman," said a man. "And his valet. Poxy fellow, he is. Smells bad, as if he was dead two weeks and rotting. But he seems lively enough. He can drink any of us under the table."

Semyon remembered the lingering odor of decay in the room. His heightened senses, all ten of them, had brought him hence for a reason.

"Really," he said. "Point him out if he comes in. I wager I can outdrink him. Or any other man here."

"Can you?" said the stout man, sitting up straighter at the mention of a bet. "He has just come in."

Semyon looked to where he nodded and saw a middle-aged man, not very tall but strongly built, come in and take a table by himself. Making haste to serve him, the barmaid brought him a bottle of whiskey and a short glass.

"Ah, well. Bet's off if it's whiskey. Makes my head swim. I thought it was ale you meant."

"No." The stout man seemed to lose interest if a wager was not to be and went back to what was left of his meal.

Semyon rose and bid them a good day, walking to the door in an easy way, as if he had nothing better to do. The closer he came to the man, the more his blood raced.

Whoever he was, he had had his hands on Angelica. The thought infuriated Semyon. The man drinking whiskey was too ugly and too uncouth for her to have gone off with him willingly. Semyon wondered what gentleman employed him.

He knew he was close to her. Very close. The tavern doors

opened to admit another laborer and Semyon pushed past him.

Outside he could see what was left of the open field surrounding the too-new-looking houses. It was a bleak prospect and the street had the look of a stage set in a provincial production. Not all the houses had glass installed and the wind whistled through those in a mournful way.

Semyon looked at the one in the center, which had not only glass but curtains behind them. Idly, he wondered why. Besides the men building here, there didn't seem to be neighbors who might spy or intrude. It was the perfect place to—

Hide someone.

Again his instincts took over. His entire body thrummed with awareness, alert to the unseen presence of the woman he sought. Semyon fingered the slip of paper in his pocket, his only physical connection to Angelica.

It was warm, but then it had been in his pocket, close to his body. Semyon walked on, wanting a back view of the house with curtains. His boots scuffed in the dirt of the unpaved street—he was grateful for the dry weather. Rain would have turned the street into a river of mud.

A hack carriage rattled behind him, less noisy than usual because its wheels were going over dirt and not cobblestones. He turned around as it pulled up in front of the house with curtains.

One twitched. Behind it, for a fraction of a second, he glimpsed Angelica. He was thunderstruck and only just refrained from shouting to her. He gazed up at her frightened face as she stepped backward into the room she was in and he lost sight of her.

Another movement, in the street this time, caught his eye. The so-called valet was returning from the bar. Semyon went behind a half-finished wall to spy upon him, watching him go in to the house where Angelica was.

Not a minute later, a different man came out, dressed like a rich young buck, tall and strong, wearing polished boots and gentlemanly attire.

Jealousy hit Semyon again. Had she gone off with this popinjay in the night?

It was none of his business if she had, he told himself. And if the fellow was single, he might be more worthy of her time than a married lecher like Congreve. He could not judge her. Indeed, he and all his brethren were thought of as outsiders. They consorted mostly with free-spirited women with reputations and left the innocents and husband-hunters alone.

He turned his thoughts to Angelica again, reminding himself of the wary sadness in her eyes as she stood in the curtained room. This time, he had seen pure terror.

She had been asleep and alone. It could well be that she had been brought to this distant part of London by force. Such things did happen.

The gentleman, if he was that, got into the carriage, which turned in the street and went toward the heart of London. That left, as far as Semyon knew, the valet in the house. There could be many other servants there. He could not just storm the gates and take her. He had to talk to her first.

He came out from behind the wall and walked on, going beyond the last house of the row, striding far afield to where he could watch the house in solitude until the sun went down again.

With luck, the marks of the wolf on his body would retreat. He would need his hands and fingers more than paws. But it was growing colder. He would miss the ruff that warmed his back.

Angelica's heart was pounding when she stepped back from the window, shocked beyond measure to have seen Semyon again. How had he known where she was when she did not know herself?

She fought the wild thought that he too might be her enemy, an ally of the man who had tricked her into smelling the poisonous rose.

But the look they had exchanged did not fit that. His eyes had flashed with joy at the sight of her, then looked searchingly at the façade of the house as if he had never seen it before—and then, when her stepbrother left, he had watched Victor with the piercing yellow gaze of a wolf.

She did not remember his eyes being that color, unless they had reflected the gold curtains of the room where they'd met. No—she knew their color. They were hazel.

Though she'd withdrawn behind the curtains by then, out of his view, she had still been able to see him and she remembered the bright flash in Semyon's eyes when he'd seen Victor get into the hack carriage and drive off. Then she watched, her heart sinking, as he'd walked away, soon out of sight once and for all.

Distraught, half-starved by now, she crawled upon the bed and cried as if her heart would break.

A new moon curved in the sky when she opened her eyes again, vanishing over the horizon when she closed them, praying for sleep that would not come.

Victor had not returned to her locked chamber and no one had come for the tray of food. She was infinitely weary, thinking sluggishly of how she might gain her freedom and letting her thoughts drift.

With the last of her strength ebbing away and no help, she could not do it. Better to bide your time, she told herself. Eat. Accept the inevitable.

She heard footsteps, quiet ones, so quiet that she thought she was imagining them. Angelica trembled.

The doorknob turned soundlessly and the key moved inside the lock with the faintest of clicks.

Her subdued wrath returned full force and she looked around for something to smash into Victor's face, whirling around frantically when the door opened to see—

Semyon. With a finger to his lips.

She took hold of a chair to steady herself.

He beckoned to her.

She shook her head.

With swift strides, stealthy and quiet as a wild animal, he closed the distance between them. "You must come with me," he whispered urgently. "The other man is asleep—there are no curtains on his windows."

"How could you see that with only a new moon in the sky?" But she wanted to believe him. Needed to.

"I cannot tell you how, but I did. Come, Angelica. We may be discovered any moment!"

"Why should I trust you?" She was shaking violently.

"You must. You did not come here willingly. You were taken. I know it."

Again she shook her head in refusal, paralyzed with fear.

Semyon stretched out a hand and she surprised herself by taking it. His fingers were warm and an indefinable strength flowed through them and into her own. Little by little, her courage came back.

Just enough to take a step toward him.

He swept her into his arms and carried her down the stairs and out the door to a waiting carriage. A black one, unembellished but costly in appearance, with drawn shades. The driver slapped the reins against the horses' rumps and they were off. He gathered her to him and enfolded her in a soft blanket, and then in his arms.

"Who are you?" she whispered. "Where are we going?"

"You know my name."

She rested her head wearily against his chest as he stared straight ahead through the little window that let the passengers view the road.

"Yes, I do. Have I gone from the frying pan into the fire?"

"If you are asking if I am a man like the one who took you in the night, the answer is no."

"But you have a reputation for your wicked way with women."

"Bah. I have never forced a woman. And I never would."

She nestled a little closer. "How did you find me? Why did you want to?"

"Instinct."

Angelica pondered that terse reply. "Is that your answer to both of my questions?"

He kissed the top of her head, smoothing her hair with one hand. "Yes."

"Will you let me go free?"

He made a demurring sound in his throat. "If you want to. I think you should stay with me for your own safety for a time."

She made no reply to that, bewildered by all that happened and weak from hunger and thirst. Her stomach constricted sharply as they rounded a corner and Angelica gagged.

He wrinkled his nose. Even she could smell the bile in her mouth. He raised a side window. "Spit," he commanded her. "And do not be a lady about it."

She obeyed and sank back against the cushions, wiping her mouth, knowing that she must look a fright.

"How long since you have eaten, Angelica?"

"I don't know," she murmured. "I don't know how long I was there. I woke up in an empty room with an iron shackle around my ankle, chained to the wall."

His jaw tightened and a look of pure fury flashed in his eyes. "Then he does deserve to die."

She went on, feeling oddly unemotional. "I was moved from there after I fainted. My new prison was much nicer—fit for the mistress of a wealthy man, I thought."

"Angelica—"

"But the door was locked and it was still a prison. I was alone. Victor sent up a maid with a tray but I would not touch the food."

"Then you must promise me that you will eat when I have you safely settled," Semyon said.

She nodded, nothing more.

"So your captor's name is Victor. Do you know his last name? Or the name of the other man, his valet?"

Struck with sudden terror, overwhelmed by her compelling shame at her stepbrother's malevolent ill-use of her and threats of worse, she shook her head.

She could not, would not, tell Semyon one single word of the ugly truth. Yes, she had gone with him and would stay with him for a time, regain her strength, even sleep with him if he wished it. She owed him that much.

Then, someday soon, she would set out on her own again. To a new land, where no one she knew would bother to find her. America. Or Canada. Or to Australia on the other side of the globe. She felt no more worthy than a convict, ready to sentence herself to transportation and permanent exile to escape her past. It didn't matter to her. But this gallant man, her rescuer, deserved better.

She was too damaged for him.

Two days later . . .

Semyon had brought Angelica to a pretty little house in a Mayfair mews, well-hidden from the street, which he said was owned by a friend of his. There were no servants and she needed none. She had *been* one, after all.

Angelica had refrained from inquiring about where he actually lived, given her own reluctance to tell him anything about herself. She asked no questions about his family or his foreign name, remembering in a vague way from the gossip she'd heard that he had two brothers, rakes once, married now.

So be it.

She and Semyon would play at domesticity for a little while themselves. He was kindness itself and the sunny little house was a sanctuary. He had opened accounts for her at the shops, and the butcher's and the grocer's, as well. She'd penned a list of what she needed and it had all been delivered. She had busied herself putting things in place, watering the potted plants that awaited the return of spring on the deep windowsills, and even befriending a stray cat that happened by.

You and I are two of a kind, she had thought while stroking the shy little animal for the first time.

She tried not to think about Victor at all. If he found her— she wondered why he would even try—Semyon would defend her somehow.

Was he as much of a rake as some claimed? Others might say he was courteous to a fault.

Not her. She felt as if she could breathe again for the first time in several years and she had him to thank for that.

Angelica started a coal fire in the little kitchen stove, coaxing it to burn brightly. She had planned a light supper for the two of them, with bought bread and chutney, but cooking the chops herself.

She straightened, coughing a bit, and looked at the clock on the mantel in the next room. Everything she needed was near to hand—the house fit her perfectly although Semyon seemed almost too big for it, especially the two upstairs rooms.

He'd declared that everything he'd bought for it was all hers. For now, she told herself. Not for always.

As the winter day faded away, she grew thoughtful, almost dreamy, sitting with the cat in her lap and waiting for him.

He had the key. She would not have to jump up and go to answer the door when he came. In another half hour, she heard him call her name from outside and knock. The dozing cat had slid off her lap and curled up elsewhere, so she did jump up and run to the door, opening it just as he was about to insert the key.

She took it from his hand and drew him inside. He pressed a chaste kiss to her forehead as she did.

"How rosy you are," he murmured. "And what have you been doing?"

"Nothing at all. I ordered chops from the butcher and I intend to cook them for you, though."

"You are ambitious."

"It is not difficult." She looked at the bottle he held. "Is that wine?"

"Yes, a French one."

"Then we shall be merry together."

He took the liberty of pulling her into his arms and giving her another kiss, not quite as chaste. The sensation of it was deeply soothing—and equally arousing. Angelica felt rather flustered.

They sat down to supper and the wine, while he told her something of his day, amusing her by imitating some of the people who'd passed through it. He had a gift for mimicry and had her laughing out loud.

How easy it was to be with him, she thought wistfully. She did not want this interlude in her life to come to an end, ever.

He stretched out to his full length on the sofa, boots propped on the arm of it because it was six inches too short, when she got up to put the kettle on for tea.

"Where are you going?" he asked in a low voice.

She told him.

"Never mind that. Come to me, Angelica. Let me hold you. It will do us both good."

She gave him a startled look. The trace of huskiness in his voice gave away his sentimental mood. He opened his arms in invitation and she went to him at once.

"Lie down," he whispered.

She dealt with her skirts first, then did just that, stretching by his side. "I fit upon the sofa nicely," she teased him.

"So you do."

She rested a hand over his heart to feel its steady beat and he covered it with his own.

"Are you happy in this house?" he asked her, stroking her hair.

"Yes, Semyon. I feel quite safe here."

He was silent and she looked up at him. His thoughtful expression and faraway look intrigued her, and she reached up a hand to caress his strong jaw. He turned to see her better.

Angelica's lips parted on a soft inward breath. In another second, he had rolled on his side, drawn her close, and was kissing her madly.

Chapter 5

Semyon seemed to know exactly what she wanted. His sensuality was no longer restrained, yet he was gentle. His mouth covered hers, kissing her with luxurious slowness, allowing her to soften to him. His hands moved over her in ardent caresses that made her arch, pressing against him with an awakened passion that burned away every trace of her recent terror.

Purely physical sensation filled her body. She had no words for what she felt, did not want to speak. He murmured endearments and she kissed him in reply, savoring the taste of him, her lips to his lips, his strong jaw, his neck—she buried her face there, inhaling the warm naturalness of his arousal.

He bent his leg to bring his thigh between hers, parting them with deliberate pressure. She wanted so to yield completely to him and she knew this was only the beginning. Still lying by his side, Angelica opened to him, and clasped her thighs around his.

He began a slow, rocking motion with his hips, sending rhythmic quivers of pleasure through her. Angelica responded instinctively to it, moving as he did, moaning almost inaudibly into his eager mouth.

He acknowledged her tiny cries with more kisses, sliding his hand down over her bodice and caressing her breasts ever so lightly through the fine pleats of linen. The sensual friction was highly exciting. Her nipples grew tight and hard against the soft linen as he cupped each one in turn, bending his head lower to nibble at her ear.

That she had seen lovers do, but never had she experienced it. He suckled tenderly on one plump little lobe, his breath warming her hair as he pushed it back. It was easy to imagine what he would do to her erect nipples—she craved the expert stimulation he would give those.

Ah, dear God . . . to feel a male mouth clasped tight around one and gently tugging fingers on the other . . . and a hot tongue-tip licking at the nipple in his lips. Dreamily, lost in a heated daze, she wondered how to tell him that this was her first time.

It was a gift indeed, that it should be with a lover of his caliber.

"May I look at you?" he whispered in her ear. "Just your breasts at first. We shall not hurry."

She fumbled with the tiny buttons set into the pleats, then felt surer, stronger fingers take over as he flicked each one free of its little hole. His hand slid under the bodice but over the chemise beneath that, using its even finer, almost transparent linen to stimulate her nipples.

His masterful expertise brought her to the point of sighing rapture. She wanted to tear away the delicate linen, remove the last fragile barrier to his exploring hands.

He seemed to know that she might, for he clasped her wrist when her fingers curled around the lace frill at the top of the chemise, ready to rend it and fully bare her breasts.

"Let me," she panted. "I want nothing between us—oh, Semyon—"

"Not yet." His voice was low. With a deep breath, he swung up to a half-sitting position and moved her on her back, straddling her hips, dominant yet gentle.

"Oh!"

She looked up, gasping, resting her hands on the spread, breeches-clad thighs to either side of her. He was magnificent, his dark eyes half-hidden by long lashes, looking down to drink in the sight of her beneath him, pressed down into the yielding cushions of the sofa.

A slow, somewhat wicked smile curled his mouth as he took her hands and pressed a kiss into the palm of each one. Then he set them underneath his knees and she understood.

He wanted her to permit him sensual liberties without her having to respond. The thought was deeply exciting. She arched at the waist and thrust her aching breasts upward.

With a sigh of anticipation, he rested his hands upon them for the briefest of moments, circling and rubbing with extraordinary skill. Pinned, she could do nothing but accept his loving caress and let the sensation itself take over.

He stopped but only to lick the forefinger and thumb on each hand, wetting the linen of her chemise until it was transparent in the two spots he chose over the nipples beneath, pink and proud. He tugged at each simultaneously, rolling them in his fingers, watching her face.

Angelica wanted to close her eyes and simply experience the intense pleasure he was giving her, but she wanted to see him just as much. His skillful manipulation of her nipples overcame her soon enough and her eyelids fluttered shut as she begged him not to stop.

The bulge in his breeches grew larger, heavy balls drawn

tight and squeezed around the base of a splendid erection. All she knew of that was not from her own experience, but a glimpse or two of pictures from a mistress's erotic album and the lewd chatter among housemaids. She had never seen a man completely naked.

Breathless, writhing between the powerful legs that held her down, she knew that Semyon would be beautiful in an utterly masculine way.

She pulled her hands free and put one boldly on the front of his breeches. The smooth leather was hot to the touch and the rod it barely restrained throbbed under her fingertips. She stroked its length once . . . then twice. Then she cupped both her hands over it and squeezed, hoping that her inexperienced caress would please him.

Semyon drew in his breath and bit his lip. "I shall explode—don't—I beg of you!"

She put her hands on his thighs again and studied him. His face was flushed with arousal and a faint sheen of sweat glistened on his neck.

In one swift move, Semyon stretched up to pull his shirt free of his breeches, then lowered his arms and crossed them, yanking at the hem and pulling it over his head. He threw the shirt on the floor, not moving out of his straddling position atop her, and put his hands on his hips, his torso heaving with rapid breaths.

The position made the muscles and tendons in his arms swell out strongly, as he was made of oak and iron. His chest had a sprinkling of fine dark hair from shoulder to shoulder that narrowed into a trailing line down his taut, powerfully muscled belly. She let her gaze move wantonly over him and saw his small nipples grow tight and turn a darker shade of brown when she had not even touched them.

She wanted to. Half naked, he was glorious. What was to

come . . . she wanted that too, wanted all of him. But he seemed to care nothing for his own body, only hers.

Once his breathing had slowed, he reached forward again, easing the chemise down so that her breasts were bared at last. He was so tall that he had to slide his hips down to suck at her nipples, and the long rod she had clasped with such delight now pressed against her most intimate flesh. He could not help but rub a little, charged with sexual need.

Angelica ran her fingers into his hair, loving the thick wildness of it, holding his head as he suckled her nipples with abandoned intensity, cupping the soft flesh of her breasts in his hands and squeezing them together so that he could take both nipples at once into his mouth. He nipped and licked at them, squeezing, pressing, giving a growl when she cried out with pleasure.

Then he sat up again, breathing harder now.

Angelica felt bereft and her breasts were cold. Without thinking, she cupped them in her hands.

"Yes," he said huskily. "Oh yes."

Again she understood what he wanted with no more explanation than that. She began to pet and stroke her breasts while he watched, drawing her palms in circles over the erect nipples, arching to enjoy the erotic friction of skin on skin in just those two small spots. Then she clutched them, hard, surprising him.

His eyes widened. "You are rough with yourself, Angelica."

"It feels good now," she whispered. She let go, though, but only to take the nipples in her fingers. More vigorously than he had done, she tugged at them, pinching firmly until they were scarlet. She wanted them to hurt a bit, so that he could soothe them with his loving mouth. Her handling of herself seemed to drive him half-mad. In another moment, he pushed her hands away and took the reddened tips into his mouth, one after the other.

He stopped, gasping against her neck, and lifted his hips away from her, cursing under his breath.

"What is wrong?"

"Nothing. You excite me beyond belief." He rose, almost staggering to a chair and sat down, yanking at his boots. They hit the floor and he reached for the button at his waistband, hesitating when he looked at her. He slid it free but stopped.

"You first, my beauty."

Feeling utterly wanton, thinking of nothing else but him and what they were about to do, Angelica merely looked at him and began to slide her skirts up her legs. Her slippers were long since off, fallen to the floor in the first moves of their sensual game. But her stockings remained. Above the knees, she was entirely naked.

She moved the skirt higher. And higher still.

His eyes feasted eagerly upon every inch of what she was showing him, and his lips parted with delight when the linen dragged over the nest of curls at the apex of her thighs.

Shyly, as she had sometimes done under the covers when entirely alone, she slid a finger in that warm little place. Watching him as he watched her, she slid it over the bud at the top, flicking it until it stood forth from the damp curls.

Forgetting all about his buttons, Semyon stood up and came instantly to kneel beside her, not looking at her face, kissing the tiny bud and drawing it into his mouth.

Dear God. A hot wave of pulsing sensation shot through her, again and again. This was not something she could do for herself.

Semyon parted her thighs, pushing the folds of her skirt up to her waist. He was far less controlled now, on fire with lust at the sight and smell and taste of her most intimate flesh. He lifted her leg and draped it over his broad back, spreading her nether lips gently with his fingers.

She moaned, abandoning herself to pleasure she'd never dreamed of in her solitary and tentative explorations. The tongue that had licked at her nipples now applied itself to her clitoris, lapping on each side, then the tip, then swirling around the whole bud as he took it in his mouth.

Now . . . now . . . The word echoed in her mind. She could not tell him that these delirious sensations were new to her. That she was an untried innocent. Dear God. He would not believe *that*.

She was too overcome to say or do anything, devoured by a lusting mouth that wanted only to give her pleasure so intense she was about to dissolve.

His large hands slid under her buttocks and began to squeeze them strongly, pushing them together, then apart, bouncing her bottom in a naughty, extremely exciting way. He left off his tongue-play upon her bud, catching his breath and wiping his wet mouth on the inside of her thigh.

He nipped at that soft flesh as she rolled wantonly in his hands, crying his name.

Then he stopped everything. Angelica opened her eyes, not knowing that she'd shed tears until he wiped them away, looking at her.

"Tell me what you want," he said. "I can hold back—you must come first."

"More." She breathed the single word. "More."

He nodded, obedient to her desire, and bent his head between her legs once more. With even greater care, he spread open the flushed, swollen lips of her sex and then . . . slid the tip of his tongue between them.

He lapped a little, then probed deeper. Angelica tensed. The tip of his tongue touched the intact membrane of her hymen. He seemed to be testing it, but only for a few seconds, as if he had not expected it to be there at all.

The feeling was strangely sensual but she felt a flash of fear. Would he be angry that she had not told him she was a virgin?

Semyon withdrew, looking at her confusedly. "Am I— your first lover, Angelica?"

"Yes," she said in a whisper, trembling all over.

"Are you sure—"

"I want it to be you," she said passionately. "I know it in my soul, Semyon."

She tore at her clothes as he tried to still her, fighting him until she was naked. "Now," she whispered, laying back. His lovemaking had stripped away her defenses and her self-restraint. And every trace of her shame.

"Angelica—" he said wonderingly, gazing at her with astonished tenderness.

She sat up and yanked at his half-undone waistband. Semyon did not defend himself, just let the buttons fly and the breeches drop. He stepped out of them and stood before her in all his erect magnificence.

"Now!"

He came over on all fours, his long, stiff cock too erect to bob. She reached for it, stroking the heated, silky skin as if she'd been born knowing how to pleasure him.

"I want you in me!"

"Angel, we must go slowly," he pleaded.

She lifted her knees with her hands and spread herself completely open. He looked down and then up, a bit dazed.

"I cannot wait," was all she said as she pulled him down to her.

He grasped the shaft and handled it urgently, tugging down the furled tip of his foreskin. Then he positioned the plumlike head where his tongue had so recently been.

"Now?" he asked desperately

She clung to his shoulders, bucked her hips, and took him herself with an upward thrust that enfolded him. "Ah! Ah, yes, Semyon!" she cried.

And they were one.

Chapter 6

"Ivan, where is Antosha?"

The housemaster gave him a disapproving look as Semyon strolled through the front door and shut it behind him. "In the front parlor, scribbling away. Do you never wear a hat?"

"No." Semyon headed for the parlor.

"It is winter. You will catch your death of cold. Do you not fear a case of catarrh?"

"Not at all. I find frigid weather exhilarating," Semyon said cheerfully. He glanced in the mirror and ran a hand through his hair, hopelessly messy from both the wind outside and Angelica's eager caresses during their dawn lovemaking. He particularly wanted to remember the last and he would not comb it.

He turned from his reflection toward the door to the parlor as Ivan held up a hand. "Stop for a moment. May I ask why you want to talk to him? You have never shown the slightest interest in his work as a secretary."

"Forgive me. I find meetings boring beyond belief, from

first to last, and I wish Antosha would not slog through detailed minutes of the previous one for the benefit of those who slept through it."

"Like you," the housemaster pointed out. "The late hours you keep are no excuse. Sometimes you don't come home at all."

Semyon ignored the jab. "And he also insists on presenting a long-winded summation at the end."

"It is unkind of you to yawn so conspicuously when he does," Ivan said acidly.

"Then I will apologize to him directly."

Semyon knew the housemaster had been charged with keeping him in line during his brothers' sojourns elsewhere. It occurred to him that the older man might feel a twinge of jealousy as well because of Semyon's easy friendship with his young wife Natalya. It was best to be tactful, he decided.

"And as far as his magnum opus, Ivan," he continued, "I am sure it is excellently written, and even more sure that Antosha's year-to-date purchases of paper and ink are generating substantial profits for the manufacturers of both. All in all, a worthy endeavor."

Ivan only sniffed.

"But I am not sure that the history of the Pack of St. James should be made public."

The housemaster raised his eyebrows. "Antosha has assured me that your after-hours pastimes will not be included."

"I beg your pardon?"

"Semyon, you have the worst reputation of all the Taruskins and you are not at all discreet. Have you considered that your affairs could reflect badly on the Pack as a whole?"

That could be said of many of his kinsmen. Semyon was indignant. "What of it, Ivan? Shall I become a monk?"

"Don't be ridiculous."

"Then what do you expect of me?" Semyon pressed him.

"I am merely reminding you that every dalliance carries an element of risk," Ivan said primly.

Semyon folded his arms across his chest and stood his ground, a challenging look in his eyes. "On that, Ivan, we agree—more than you know. But I am my own man and the matters of my heart are my concern, not yours."

The housemaster gave a sigh and shot a narrow look at Semyon. "Who is it this time?"

"I don't know what you're talking about."

"Grisha and Todt and Vladimir told me you have set them to guard a little house in Mayfair."

"Oh, that." Semyon uncrossed his arms and began to pace. "It belongs to a friend of mine."

"Then why must our men watch the place? I don't suppose they are guarding the geraniums in the windows," Ivan added thoughtfully.

"No, they are not."

"Cagey, aren't you? They say they have seen no one come and go through its door save you."

"Then there is nothing to worry about, is there, Ivan?"

The other man harrumphed, clearly not satisfied with that answer.

Semyon checked his rising temper and reminded himself that the junior members of the Pack, including those three, were obliged to report on their activities. He himself was entitled to a freedom that they had not yet earned. But he cursed silently for forgetting to instruct them to say nothing of the Mayfair house just yet.

Not that he would ask them to lie. But he honestly did not expect Angelica to stay there long. In her demure way, she was as wild as a wolfess. He had not seen a forever-after look in her beautiful eyes, even when she'd lain so blissfully in his arms after a night, a day, and another night of lovemaking.

He had yet to ask her to reveal the details of her strange abduction. She seemed to have placed all her trust in him, as if his claiming of her virginity had magically taken away her fear. With her in his arms, open-hearted and passionate, then, vulnerable in slumber, he felt like a champion.

In idle moments he entertained a fantasy he had no wish to share with her: finding out the full name of her captor and whether he had accomplices. There were criminal rings that kidnapped women, to be sure, and girls and youths, most of whom disappeared into the rookeries and brothels of London's slums, never to be seen again.

He knew where the man lived, but nothing else. He suspected there were others involved besides the fellow named Victor. So far his inquiries had turned up nothing of substance and he had no leads.

He had asked a contact in the department of property records to look up the deeds for the new development. There were not that many and none had been issued to someone with the first name of Victor.

Since Angelica would not tell him more at the moment, or was not yet ready to, he had to investigate on his own.

"Is there anything else you wished to talk to me about?" he asked Ivan, peaceably enough.

"No. Do as you please."

The older man stalked away, going about his business as Semyon headed for the front parlor.

He raised his hand to knock on the closed door and noted absently that it was rather furry. It had not been last night. No matter. The marks of the wolf in him sometimes came and went.

"Come in," Antosha said.

Semyon turned the knob and entered. The front room was flooded with sunlight that only heightened the secretary's pallor. Did the man never go outside?

"Scribble, scribble, scribble, eh? You never stop," Semyon said jokingly. "How goes the book?"

"Slowly." Antosha finished the sentence he was setting down, blotting his meticulous handwriting with care as Semyon settled himself in a chair and watched a bit impatiently. "I am five pages away from the conclusion."

"Bully for you, Ant. What are you going to call it?" he asked.

"*The Complete History of the Trans-Asiatic Wolf Clans and Their Genealogical Antecedents, with Appendices.*"

"Quite a mouthful." Semyon pondered for a few seconds, scratching the bothersome stubble on his chin. "You will not sell one copy with a title like that."

"It is a scholarly work," Antosha said quietly, taking off his spectacles and folding the earpieces in.

"There is nothing wrong with making money, is there? I understand you have worked night and day upon it for a year or more."

"I have," Antosha said with a gloomy sigh.

"Then call it something else or it will languish at the bookseller's. Something thrilling if you want to entice readers to buy it. And do leave out the long words."

Antosha shook a tiny drop of ink from the nib and chewed absentmindedly on the end of his pen for a few moments. "Hmm. I suppose I could call it *The Thrilling Tale of the Pack of St. James, and the Dangerously Dashing Taruskin Brothers.* Would that do?"

"Yes." Semyon laughed at the secretary's sly answer. "A definite improvement, I think." He was glad that Antosha was in a good mood, because he had a favor to ask of him. "Truly, I look forward to reading it."

Antosha gave him a considering look. "But you are rarely here."

Semyon acknowledged that with a nod. He had no wish to

argue with the secretary as he had with the housemaster. "Alas, that is true. And there is only one copy. But I will read it someday, I promise you, Antosha."

The secretary studied him in silence for several moments. "May I ask why you are buttering me up, Semyon?" he finally said.

"I am not," he replied indignantly. "But I did want to ask you something. If you have finished the book, then perhaps you will have time to help me."

"Let's hear it." Antosha leaned back in his spindly chair.

"On behalf of a friend."

"Female friend," the secretary said. "It is always a female with you Taruskins."

Semyon coughed. "It does not matter. But I need to find out who owns a certain piece of property—"

"Speculating in real estate, are you?"

Semyon made a move with his head that fell precisely between an affirmative nod and a negative shake.

"You are a true Londoner," the secretary went on. "I suppose you want to put down roots here."

"I have, Antosha. We all have."

The other man sighed wistfully. "I dream of Saint Petersburg myself. The canals. The Nevsky Prospect. Glorious architecture right and left."

"You will freeze your nose off if you go back." Semyon emphasized his point by slapping the table. "As if London wasn't cold enough."

He noticed that Antosha was looking curiously at his hand and he looked at it himself. It was more furry now than when he had knocked on the door and the fingers above the second knuckles had begun to come together to form a paw.

"Londoner or not," the secretary said, "the marks of the wolf are stronger in you than any of us."

Semyon felt faintly dismayed. "Is it that noticeable?"

"Sometimes, yes." Antosha scrutinized the rest of him. "Have you noticed that the appearance of the traits coincides with anything else? What you eat, perhaps? Or your mental state?"

Semyon preferred to admit to nothing. His occasional predawn strolls through the market and hunger for meat, his protective instincts causing his ruff to rise when Angelica had been in immediate danger—he didn't want either mentioned in Antosha's big, thick book, even if the secretary used a pseudonym for him.

"I am always the same," he replied vaguely. Antosha would have to be satisfied with that.

"Indeed," the secretary murmured. "Anyway, what was it you wanted my help with?"

"Ah, yes. Thank you for reminding me," Semyon said. "There is a new development at the end of—" he named the street. "But I cannot find out who financed it or who holds the master deed to the land. The new houses can and have been bought and sold, but the owners only lease the land underneath them. It is an odd arrangement."

"Not unheard of, however."

Semyon acknowledged that with a brief nod. "But it is an oddly lonely place, Antosha."

"That is no crime."

"If there have been people brought there against their will and kept there under mysterious circumstances, then crimes are being committed."

"Any particular person? Someone I would know?"

Semyon shook his head firmly.

"I understand. The utmost discretion is advised, et cetera, and you have already made your swaggering, handsome self too conspicuous by playing a hero, and you need a nonentity with a forgettable face, meaning me, to take it from there."

Semyon looked at the secretary with surprise. "I would not

have put it in those words, but I need help, Antosha. You seem to like digging through musty old books and records."

Antosha gave him a wry little smile. "Yes. I do."

"Then . . ."

The secretary got to his feet and put on his spectacles, tidying the items on his desk. "Just tell me where to look first, Semyon. It will be a diversion from this damned book."

"Thank you. You have my undying gratitude. And I shall order a case of the best bottled stout for you straightaway."

"I prefer sherry." Antosha named the vintage.

Semyon blanched when he heard it. "You have refined tastes, my friend. That is the very best. And worth every penny," he added hastily. "Please let me know as soon as you have found something."

It was a few days later that the two men met again. Antosha brought Semyon to his desk and took out a fair copy in his own handwriting.

"I began with a chained ledger that the property-records clerk would not permit me to remove. The volume was dusty, but there were new entries in it, as I suspected."

Semyon tried to read the minute handwriting but failed. "What did you find out?"

"Many things. I had to cross-reference my initial discoveries. But I do have the name of the man who owns the land and the houses."

"Is it Victor?"

Antosha looked at Semyon over his spectacles. "No. Why do you ask that?"

"It was all I had to go on."

"Hmm. No, the man whose identity you seek has a different given name, quite ordinary and forgettable, that he has not used for years. His alias is much more intriguing."

"Can you not just tell me?" Semyon was a little exasperated by the secretary's refusal to come to the point.

Antosha set down the paper in his hand. "In a moment. He is a notorious criminal, it seems."

Semyon shrugged, as if that did not surprise him. "And his name?" he asked again, with even less patience.

"St. Sin."

Chapter 7

Angelica looked out the window, hoping to see the stray cat that came to the house in the morning. It was already afternoon and there had been no sign of the animal, her sole companion when Semyon was not with her.

She sighed, wishing he would return. Like any other man of means, he had business affairs to attend to, she supposed.

Still . . . as far as she was concerned it was in the bedroom where he excelled. Her first night with him and the day after were still vivid in her mind. Her sexual initiation had been spectacular, his prowess as a lover unmatched, she was sure.

If she were to have just one man in all her life, she would want that man to be him.

Angelica knew how unlikely that pretty dream was. Worthy men, successful men, did not seek to marry women like her.

No family. No fortune. Landing wherever the wind seemed to blow her, and not always on her feet. Her luck, such as it was, would last as long as her beauty did.

Moving restlessly through the small rooms of the borrowed house, she paused in front of a mirror, taking stock of her appearance. She smoothed her gown, and then her hair, not liking the disarray of either and too nervous to correct it.

A faint scratching at the window announced the return of the cat and she stepped outside in her dress and thin slippers to bring it in to sit with her.

"And where have you been?" The cat seemed to grow tamer by the day, nestling belly up in her arms as she went back through the door. It purred. "I hope you have not been keeping company with that ugly old tom I saw on the back fence. I heard those yowls. No kittens, if you please."

She set it down upon the sofa, where it kneaded the cushions before curling up and going to sleep.

There was nothing to do in the house, and Semyon, thoughtful as he was, had not bought books to read or other diversions.

Indeed, there had not been time to see to such little comforts and she felt she had no right to complain of her confinement.

She stroked the sleeping cat, wishing she had its freedom to come and go. Soon enough, she supposed, Semyon would tire of her and this love nest. Still, it was pleasant to be mistress of a house and have him as her master.

He had thought to provide her with dresses and undergarments, not made to order but they all fit perfectly and were new. His taste ran to low-cut and diaphanous things, although there had been a shawl or two, and a thick cloak in the huge trunk of clothes when it arrived. So many clothes that she had not had time to go through them all.

She had no idea what, if anything, he planned for the two of them. But Angelica did feel safe in the mews house. He had finally told her of the guards who kept watch over her, of course. They kept themselves out of her sight—she had never so much as glimpsed any of the three.

Well, then. If she had no book to read or piano to play, she might as well mend the dress and chemise she had ripped so wantonly. The memory of that passionate moment cheered her up. She had hung both garments in the clothespress, gathering the buttons in a small bag, and asked him for thread and needles to be delivered.

Like so much else in the house, a sewing case had been set on the doorstep for her to find just yesterday. That too was in the clothespress.

She went upstairs and brought it all to a sunny window, pulling up a chair for herself. Pins in her mouth, she hummed to herself, sewing for at least an hour and glad for a bit of work to pass the time and occupy her mind.

In the darkest corner of it lurked vile memories of her stepbrother, and her nightmarish confinement. Thinking of him, even for a second, made her hands unsteady. A pin pricked the pad of her thumb and she set her sewing aside, sucking the blood from it. The light-colored dress and chemise would stain from the tiniest drop.

In time the small wound sealed itself but she had lost interest in what she was doing. Her restlessness returned like a plague upon her soul.

Angelica stuffed the half-repaired garments back into the clothespress and went to look in the trunk. Semyon had advised her to stay in the house and she had agreed not to show her face out-of-doors.

Wearing a veil would help her keep that hasty promise. Had whoever filled the trunk thought to include one? She dragged it forth and lifted the lid to rummage through it, setting various articles of clothing into heaps.

There was a shawl of gossamer gray wool, thin and extremely fine, that would do, she thought. She rose and wrapped it around her head, then pulled the last part over her face. It was quite easy to see through. She went to the mirror and gave a start.

The material gave her a ghostly look, but that couldn't be helped. She had barely recognized herself for a moment.

Angelica took it off and tossed other things on the bed—a warn wool overdress, the cloak, and a scarf to secure her improvised veil. In another few minutes she was dressed and peering outside her door, feeling adventurous and a little frightened.

She glimpsed her reflection in the windowpane when she stepped outside, and satisfied herself that she could not be recognized, thinking that she looked almost like a novitiate of some unknown order of nuns.

It is only for an hour or two, she told herself. Semyon had said he would not return before nightfall. He did not need to know.

She looked up and down the street leading out from the mews, and saw no one. The afternoon sun slanted in large bars through the bigger houses surrounding the mews, but it gave little warmth. Angelica turned up the collar of the cloak for good measure and walked out.

It was a pleasure indeed to be free—and in her odd guise, ignored by men and women alike. She had not realized that the mews house was so near one of the main streets of Mayfair, and the hustle and bustle of people hurrying along was exactly what she'd needed.

She lingered at an interesting shop window now and then, but never for very long, not wanting to be invited in by a proprietor, no matter what was in the window. The routine of other people's days, people she did not know and never would, was a distraction and a comfort.

A bench in a secluded spot attracted her and she went to it, her feet aching from walking on cobblestones. She pulled the cloak tightly around herself, wishing the bench were in a sunnier place. Still, it was amusing to watch the hubbub, now mostly goodwives and mothers and housemaids come out to find something they needed to cook for dinner, judging by the contents of the baskets over their arms.

Inside her cloak was a reticule with a few coins. But Angelica did not want to take the risk of being remembered by ordering anything to eat or drink in a public place. Feeling a bit chilly, she got up and walked farther down the lane that meandered away from the bench, spying a church at the end of it.

She was not religious but sitting in churches to think was something she had always done. A long-ago friend, a Catholic, had brought her along on a Sunday now and then and sometimes on a Saturday to attend confession, despite her mother's disapproval.

The elaborate rites of communion and the intonations in Latin had baffled her, but Angelica hadn't minded. Even the lingering smell of incense on her clothes, which had shocked her mother most of all, was pleasant to her.

Peering through the veil she found it difficult to determine just what sort of church it was and walked closer. Workmen were coming out the door, removing statues and other articles that she vaguely remembered as similar to the ones in her friend's church.

"What are you doing?" She hadn't realized she'd spoken the question aloud until one of the workmen answered her.

"What we are paid to do, miss. The church is bein' deconsecrated," he said. "The notice is posted there." He pointed. "It was sold, you see."

It had never occurred to her that a church could be sold, but she supposed it was a building like any other. She looked up at the carvings of the evangelists and wondered if she looked as sad as they did.

When the going in and out seemed to have ended, she went inside and sat in a pew. Those, she supposed, might stay. The nave was empty but illuminated by the last rays of sunlight. Simply to sit there made her feel at peace, though it brought back poignant memories of more innocent days.

Angelica saw a movement in the shadows even through the veil and turned to it before she remembered that she should attract no attention.

A tall man stood there with a kindly smile, dressed in a long black coat with a flat tie of white. A clergyman or a priest, she could not tell. He did not seem to be either, but since it had been a Catholic Church, she decided he was a priest of some kind. One did not often see them, except in the neighborhood of the Huguenot silk weavers. But that was some distance from her.

He inclined his head to her and came a little closer. Angelica saw that he was standing next to a confessional. For a moment, she envied those of his faith and their sacred rite of confession and absolution.

The thought of her stepbrother's lust for her filled her with shame. What she had done with Semyon did not. Their loving was life-giving and wondrous—she felt it had begun to heal her. Certainly he had protected her as no man had ever done.

Perhaps, she thought, looking up into the light of the empty nave, if she were able to confess her feelings Victor might never haunt her again.

She tried to put the odd idea from her mind—the rite was a sacrament, certainly—and she could not remember the words or their meaning.

Another woman, her face concealed by a hat, dashed down the aisle and into the booth. The priest—he must be one—stepped into the other side.

Angelica sat, hearing only indistinct murmurs, transfixed.

I will confess, I must . . . even if it is for no sin of my own. The thought resounded in her soul.

The woman came out, breathing into a twisted handkerchief, exuding her relief at being heard. She did not stop to say penitential prayers and carried no rosary, but Angelica did not notice either of those things. As if under a spell, she rose from the pew and went into the booth, seeing the shadow of the tall man on the other side of a pierced sheet of metal.

The words he muttered meant nothing to her, and she answered in a voice so low and rushed that she hardly heard herself.

His voice was as kind as his distant smile had been. She poured out her story, not caring if he understood or even if he absolved her.

When she was done, she pressed her hand to the pierced screen and thanked him.

He answered in Latin. She didn't understand, but she didn't care. Angelica left the booth and rushed out of the church, scarcely noticing that the light no longer filled the nave. She made her way back to the house in the mews as dusk fell over the city, feeling strangely exhilarated and very tired.

Semyon came in to find her asleep on the sofa, curled up around the cat. He lifted the cloak from her shoulders, supposing she had used it for a blanket and set it over a chair that held a fine gray shawl. The small house was drafty and the fire in the hearth had gone out. He maneuvered himself rather awkwardly around her and warmed her back for her, keeping a foot on the floor for balance and whispering sweet nonsense in her ear until she woke up.

"You!" she said, startled but still drowsy. She was suffused with an unfamiliar sense of well-being as if her secret confession and her feeling of sanctuary in this hidden house had combined to erase her past. If and when that should catch up with her . . . she refused to think about it now. Not with him here. His warm lust exhilarated her.

"Who else? Do you let anyone else in this house?' he asked indignantly.

"Only that cat."

As if it understood that two was company, the cat sprang up and jumped off to stretch and Angelica rolled around in his arms.

"No one else, milord."

He made himself more comfortable and kissed her gently.

"Do not call me that, even in jest. We are equals."

"Indeed not." She nuzzled his strong neck, feeling his pulse against her lips. "You are free to come and go," she said teasingly, "and I must stay here." She would not tell him of her brief escape nor of her confession in the strange church. It seemed almost dreamlike now, a mad impulse, really, though her heart was lighter for it.

"Not forever, Angelica."

She did not know what to say to that. His statement could be interpreted in more than one way. "Well, then. Are you expecting dinner? There is none."

He cuddled her closer. "I brought a roast chicken from the inn. And a bottle of sherry." He had deducted one from Antosha's case, knowing full well that the secretary would take him to task for it.

"You are a treasure, Semyon. And very kind to me."

After showing him her gratitude by rumpling his clothes and running her fingers through his hair and pressing eager kisses to his mouth, she pushed him off the sofa.

"Angelica—" He hit the floor with a huge thump.

"But I am very hungry. I will finish what I started after we eat."

"Very well," he grumbled, getting up and going with her to the kitchen, where they found the cat clawing at the paper and twine of the package he'd brought. He put the cat outside and it scampered away, leaving them alone together once more.

* * *

Cold and blue, the half moon streamed in through the shut windows, though the bedroom was warm. It was not the stub of a candle in the corner that heated it, but their bare, entwined bodies moving in a sensual rhythm in the bed, half-covered.

Semyon rose up on straight arms, pressing his weight into his palms and not her body as he pounded down into the cradling softness of her spread thighs. Her cunny was tight and slick around him, and she knew how much it aroused him. He thrust in again and again, eyes closed in bliss. She took the entire length of his thick cock just as blissfully, not in the least bit sore only a few days after her first penetration by his magnificent shaft.

Her hands slid down from his waist and over his clenched buttocks, savoring the hollows in the sides as the muscles tightened and released with every full stroke. In and out. In and out. His heavy balls touched her naked bottom every time.

She wriggled under him, bending her knees, wanting to get her legs to his shoulders, craving the deepest possible sensations he could give her.

Semyon hung his head for a moment, licking the sweat from his upper lip and gazing at her with half-closed eyes. Then he straightened, grabbed one of her ankles, then the other, getting her legs high and raising her bottom before he began again.

His body was closer to hers than before, his weight supported on his elbows and not his outstretched arms. Her breasts were bounced and squeezed in this position, her nipples brushing his hardworking chest. He moaned in appreciation each time he felt them touch, and she grew more excited, lost in mutual passion . . . until he suddenly pulled out, breathing hard.

"Why?" she murmured.

She watched him squeeze his shaft with all his strength. "So that I will not come too soon, you little cat," he gasped.

His erection did not visibly lessen, but he did not breathe as fast.

Before she could speak again, he rolled her over and lifted her gently by sliding his hands under the front of her hips. Angelica buried her face in the pillow, blushing furiously. How wanton and how natural to be on all fours with him.

He did not enter her but maneuvered until he was over her body, also on all fours.

No, threes.

He used one hand to fondle her breasts, pinching her nipples when he could catch one. The variety of sensations, coupled with the prodding erection touching her back, was marvelous. He kept it up, enjoying her cries of pleasure, lightly biting the nape of her neck and her rounded shoulders, whispering to her sensually of what he would do next.

"Then do it," she whispered back.

His hand slid down between her legs and he pleasured her cunny with two fingers held together, coming up from inside to slide them tightly over the bud of her clitoris. She muffled her delighted cries with the pillow, feeling it grow wet against her open mouth, loving everything he did to her and wanting more.

He rose up and she waited. Not patiently, but she waited.

Warm, masculine hands rested on her buttocks but she had no idea where the rest of him was. Angelica held her breath, then panted when he spread her from behind and thrust his long tongue into her throbbing slit.

That too he pushed in and out, in and out, in a rhythm so strong and sure that she felt near to climax. But without a touch to her sensitive bud, she could not.

Angelica moaned with wanton joy. She was simultaneously deeply satisfied and absolutely frustrated. He had to know it.

"Beast," she moaned. "Don't tease me so."

But his mouth was too busy cunny-kissing her to answer. His tongue probed deeply, meeting no resistance. Indeed, her innermost muscles pulled at his loving tongue, wanting all he would give her. In a little while he moved his face away from her quivering behind and she heard him roughly wipe his mouth, then felt the exposed head of his cock hot against her nether lips. He held her around the waist and slid inside her a fraction of an inch.

Again her cunny tightened with pleasure. He groaned and rammed himself in all the way, rocking against her wildly. Angelica hung on to the bed lest he fuck her to the floor, though she would not have minded that.

With a tremendous roar, he pulled out and stroked his shaft furiously, spraying hot, luxurious jets over her back and her behind.

With sobbing, happy gasps, he dropped over her and reached under to take her dripping little bud in his expert fingers, bringing her in seconds to the same heights of ecstasy he had just reached, rolling her over onto her back to kiss her lasciviously during her orgasm.

Then he collapsed to the side in utter exhaustion, drawing her to him in a tangle of sheets and sweat and come, a very satisfied beast at last.

Chapter 8

"Now then," Semyon said, watching her pour the tea the next morning, "we must decide what to do about you, Angelica."

"We must decide? Or you must decide?" she asked. She swept the floating folds of a batiste *négligé* around her and sat opposite him. Her hair was partly swept up in a loose knot and partly falling down her nape in long locks.

He looked at her fondly, patting the slippered foot she slid into his lap. "Which would you prefer, my darling?"

"That *I* decide."

He picked up his full cup with care, blowing on the surface of the hot tea to cool it. "A worthy notion, but you are without relatives to help you, or at least you have not told me of any."

A shuttered look came into her eyes and her tone grew flat. "Nonetheless—"

Semyon shook his head. "Women are dependent on men. That is the way of the world. I did not make it so, so do not scold me."

Angelica sat back in her chair. "Oh, dear. I must find pen and ink, and note this sentimental occasion in my diary. We may be on the verge of having our first quarrel."

"Really?"

She nodded her head and crossed her arms over the lacy bodice of her *négligé*. "Yes, really. Do you not agree?" she asked, until he interrupted her as she took a breath, about to speak again.

"If I agree, then we cannot be quarreling."

She heaved a sigh. "But we will be. It has begun in the usual order. A difficult question is indirectly put—"

"I don't remember asking you anything."

"You referred to my family, of which you know nothing."

He nodded and finished his tea, then held out his cup for another. She shot him a look and he ended up by pouring one for himself this time, harrumphing when he did. "If you would confide in me, that would be very helpful, Angelica."

She ignored his request. "Quarrels follow a pattern, I think." The rest of her remarks she ticked off on her fingers. "One, a difficult question is broached when the other person is off guard. Two, there is a seemingly inevitable misunderstanding. And three, the questioner retreats, only to strike again."

"I would never do such a vile thing to any woman."

Her reply was light. "Why not? The law permits it. If he is so inclined, a husband may strike his wife with a stick, so long as it is no thicker than his thumb."

"Then the law is an ass, as someone has said." He looked at her seriously. "And was your mother beaten or mistreated? I must assume that you were never married, Angelica."

"She was not. And no, I have never been married." He would have to be content with that curt answer. "But I was told of that law by my stepfather."

"So your father is dead."

He was good at putting her on the spot. She would give him a little more information as a reward of sorts. "Yes. And so is my stepfather and my mother, too. They were both taken by a virulent fever."

"And then you came to London. An orphan."

"You make it sound as if I was young enough to be left on a doorstep in a basket. I was not." She gave him a haughty look, hoping he would pry no further. "That is as much of my story as you need to know for now, Semyon. We *are* quarreling and you know it."

He smiled broadly at her, not fazed in the least by her irritable reply. "Then I hope it will be the first of many. Have some tea, Angelica. It will help you wake up properly."

She said nothing more for the moment, letting him pour her a cup. She added a few drops of milk and a bit of sugar, then drank it slowly, studying him.

He wore last night's clothes and was gorgeously disheveled. She rather liked him that way. Not shaved. His hair was extraordinarily spiky, as if he were a wild animal that had just come out of its den. It needed cutting, she thought. She wondered if he would allow her to do it. If so, she would take a lock for a keepsake. There would be little else to remember him by.

It could not be true, she told herself, that this domestic idyll would last. The sunny little house, their powerfully sensual connection, the husband-and-wife air of this morning together—none of it was permanent. She thought, studying him, that she wanted it to. But as he said, a woman alone was a vulnerable creature.

Still, she thought, she might make her escape from England and her vile stepbrother without Semyon's aid. He might beg her to stay in London, under his protection, but as long as Victor was alive, she was putting herself and Semyon at risk.

"What are you thinking?" he asked presently.

"Of what you said regarding women."

He nodded. "I would consider myself honored if you were to depend on me, Angelica."

"I fear I have already."

He straightened, sitting up tall in his chair, and considered her. "I suppose I should tell you that I have made inquiries on my own."

She pressed her lips together for a moment to compose herself. Her heart fluttered wildly in her breast. "And what have you found out?"

"The house in which you were imprisoned has a curious history, for one."

"History? But it seemed so new. And not lived in. I think it was used as a bordello—" She paused, thinking back on the bare room where she had awoken, shackled, and the other chamber, and its expensive but somehow tawdry décor.

"The man who holds the deed has an even more curious name."

She held her breath for a moment before she spoke. "Does he? What is it?" Her stepbrother's first name and last name were not common, but neither could be defined as strange. Let him tell her then, she thought warily. She would not blurt out the information.

"He is known as St. Sin."

"I have never heard of him."

Semyon nodded. "I would hope not. He is a notorious criminal, apparently, though he has never been brought before the bar."

"Why would he be?"

"He is a pimp. A common occupation, of course, and not often prosecuted."

"No," she said angrily, "some would think of such a man

as a public servant." So that was the business partner Victor had mentioned.

"It seems he is a particularly cruel one," Semyon was saying. "He is suspected of murdering more than one girl in the last several years."

"So many innocents come down to London from the country," she said softly. "The roads into London provide good hunting." She remembered the rough men and women too who had tried to steer her to houses of ill-repute. Thanks to her stepbrother, she had learned to trust no one and that alone had saved her.

Semyon nodded. "Yes. They go on the town quickly enough, many of them. It is that or starve. Poor women have little choice. For you, I suppose, it was different?"

"A leading question if ever I heard one," she said tartly.

"Angelica . . ." His voice was soothing and he took her hands in his for a moment until she pulled them away.

"What?"

"I installed you here, I bought you new clothes, I saw to it that you were guarded—I did everything I could."

"And I thank you from the bottom of my heart for it," she said honestly.

"But you knew we would have to talk about what had happened after you were taken from the Congreves' house. Where I found you—who had taken you—"

"I know no more of either than you do." That was a half lie. She was damned if she would tell him who Victor was to her. For her safety and Semyon's, her vague plan to wangle passage on a ship to another country had to happen, sooner rather than later.

"But—"

She had to stall him for now, distract him with questions of her own.

"You never did tell me how you found me, Semyon. Or why you wanted to."

He took a few moments to compose himself. Or was he inventing a lie? That was a question she dared not ask but it was not that far-fetched, Angelica thought.

"I went back to the Congreves' that same night. I wanted to see you again."

"Do you make a habit of flirting with housemaids?" The acid in her voice seemed to sting him.

"It seemed to me that you were more than that. I was dazzled by you, however brief our meeting."

"I took your coat. I smiled and nodded and you went away."

"All the same. When I returned to the ballroom, I thought that there was no woman there who compared to you in beauty and fire."

"Bah."

"It was clear to me that you were gently bred and cultured. Somehow you had come down in the world through no fault of your own. There was a sadness in your eyes—"

"Stop." Agitated, she rose from her chair and swept out of the kitchen and into the front room with the sofa.

He rose too and followed her. But he kept a little distance, as if aware of her roiling emotions. Semyon stood in the doorway with one hand upon the jamb between one room and the next, and it struck her again that the house seemed too small for him. He seemed too wild for its golden coziness as well.

"Forgive me if I say that the sadness is still there, my darling."

"And why should I not be sad? And terrified?"

"Of course—"

"I do not wish to talk of this and I have asked you to stop!"

He shook his head. "Please listen. I cannot help but observe you, although you seem determined not to give yourself away. But you are not the child of servants or raised on a farm. That is quite obvious."

"What of it?"

"I would not mind if you were, Angelica. I am only stating the obvious."

She gave a great sigh and sat on the sofa. He stayed where he was.

"I will tell you why and how I rescued you, but let me finish what I was saying."

"Go on then."

His eyes were kindly and his voice was low. "In our brief time together, when we are keeping each other amused, or when we make love—it goes away then. But it comes back."

"That is to be expected."

"If I had my way, Angelica, I would make it disappear forever."

She adjusted her position so that she did not have to look directly at him. "Forever? Nothing lasts forever. Not happiness, surely."

"My dear—"

"Semyon, I am grateful for what you have done, but do not press me to tell you everything!" she burst out. "I cannot!"

He fell silent for some moments. "But I must continue to investigate. I cannot keep you safe if I do not find out more. And you must tell me"—he hesitated—"whether you have left this house. I happened to look at the soles of the shoes you kicked off last night, the new ones I bought for you."

"Yes," she said in a small voice, "I did. I could not stand to be indoors but I took care to cover my face." She nodded toward the gray shawl on the chair. "With that. I looked odd, to be sure, but not even my own kin would have recognized me."

"And where did you go?"

"I walked about through Mayfair and when I was tired, I rested on a bench away from the main thoroughfares."

He glanced at the scarf. "Did no one stare? I cannot imagine that they did not, with a shawl wrapped about your face."

"It was cold," she said defensively. "I looked at myself to be sure my features were well hidden and thought I might be taken for a—a nun. Ridiculous, I know. But I had to go out if only for a little while."

"I understand," he said gravely, coming in to the room where she sat but not sitting down himself.

She looked up at him wistfully. "Do not judge me too harshly, Semyon."

"Never. Even though I know very little more now than I did before. I expect you will tell me when and if you are ready," he sighed.

She patted the sofa cushion. "I am sorry that I cannot. But now that we are lovers of a sort, we should not be strangers when we are together. Your presence is very comforting to me."

He raised his eyebrows and gave her a searching look, as if he was assessing the truth of her remark. "Good. That is a start." Then he sat next to her without touching her at all. "Now I will answer your questions, if I may."

"Thank you, Semyon," she said almost inaudibly.

"As I said, I went back to the Congreve house hoping to talk to you again. I was waylaid by your mistress."

He glanced at her when she frowned, studying her face.

"You did not like her, I take it."

"No one does. Not even her husband."

"Why?"

Her gaze was downcast. "Mrs. Congreve is ill-tempered and domineering. And she is a faithless wife."

"And Mr. Congreve?"

"He was amiable enough," she said tightly. "But he has a wandering eye."

"Did he pursue you?"

She smiled faintly. "Not for long. But his wife thought he did, and that I encouraged him, which was not true. And so I was demoted from lady's maid to a downstairs slavey."

"Not quite. You were too pretty for that. I suppose that is why you were given the task of seeing to the cloaks. Lady This and Lady That would not want a scullery girl with grimy fingernails handling their finery."

"Certainly not." She almost laughed, but he could see that the memory of her humiliating treatment hurt her.

He put two fingers under her chin and lifted it so that she had to look him in the face.

"Do you know what I thought when I first saw you behind that curtain?" he asked softly.

"No." The single word was a whisper.

"That I had come upon a goddess in a golden bower."

He touched a brief kiss to her lips and withdrew his hand. She didn't look away or hang her head again, As if his kiss gave her a measure of courage.

"How poetic."

"Do you always dismiss compliments so neatly, Angelica?"

She drew in her breath. "It is not as if I receive many. I will say that your awkward gallantry did please me that night."

He laughed out loud. "Your description is accurate. That was exactly how I felt."

"I thought for a moment that you might not give me your coat," she said. "You looked like you had forgotten you were holding it. And of course you had come to the wrong place."

"I followed Jack."

She wagged a finger at him. "He was in charge of the women's things."

"Perhaps I only wanted to escape the party."

"I suspect," she said slyly, "that it is more likely you wanted to dodge the eager eligibles and their ever-present mamas, and find something cool to drink into the bargain."

"There is some truth to that, Angelica," he grinned. Her intuition was remarkable. Semyon sighed inwardly. "In any case, Jack brought me to you the first time and I made my way back an hour or so later."

She gave him a wide-eyed look. "I did not know that part of the story."

"No. We have hardly talked, have we?"

Angelica moved closer to him and he drew her under his arm. "There, there. We are doing it now and that is all that needs to be said about it."

"Go on," she said, resting a hand on his chest.

"You were sound asleep on a pile of cloaks and furs and other things. I thought you were quite the most beautiful woman I had ever seen."

"In those circumstances?"

"Yes." He dropped a kiss on her hair. "I kneeled beside you, longing to caress you. But I decided to be gallant and I didn't." He was not going to tell her of his carnal fantasies when he'd watched her sleep, since she seemed to enjoy the romantic aspect of their first meeting so much. "Then Jack returned and I left. He said he would wake you. Oh—there was one other thing."

"What?"

"You were holding a rose to your lips. I was jealous, because I assumed an admirer had given it to you—"

She sat bolt upright. "That rose was poisoned. The dew in it was not dew at all. An ugly little man came in after you and he gave it to me to hold. I remember feeling sick—and swaying—I must have fallen."

"The scratches on the wall," he said. "So you did make them. I thought so."

"I tried to hold myself up. I fell, I think—and found that little book."

"So did I. I left with it, in fact."

She nodded. "After you saw I had vanished, when you came back a third time?"

"Yes. Much later, well after the party was over, as I said. Mrs. Congreve and her husband invited me in for sherry when I was standing on the street in front of the house like a lovesick fool—"

"I expect she thought you'd come back to dally with her."

"Hmm. That could be. In any case, we went into the library and both of them were soon asleep. Jack stopped me as I left and said you had vanished."

"If you could tell him that I am all right," she began hesitantly.

He patted her hand. "In due time. He was worried, but there was nothing I could do or say until I found out more. Or found you."

"And how did you do that?"

He raked a hand through his hair as he shook his head once, as if trying to find the right words.

"It is hard to explain. In my pocket was the slip of paper that you had written my name on. I held it—and I began to sense something of you."

"I see," she said. "I mean, no, I don't see at all. What are you talking about?"

He looked at her worriedly "I suppose I could say I have some, ah, instinctive skills."

Angelica looked at him warily. "Do you? But you seem the model of an English gentleman to me. Although there is something wild about you—it is a hard quality to define."

"Um. I like to hunt, like any gentleman. Perhaps that is it."

"It will have to do. But continue, please."

"When I left the Congreves'—they were snoring together—I walked the way I had come. Something, I know not what, told me to turn down a street that was not the way I would have gone. I walked for miles. And when I came to its end . . ."

He told her the remainder of his odd pursuit and night vigil in the cold, in a few short sentences. She had yet to tell him aught of her captivity.

"There you were," he finished. "You know the rest."

Overwhelmed by emotions she had choked back for all the intervening days, she buried her face in his chest and cried hot tears.

He held her closer still, murmuring endearments and reassurances. In time she quietened. He eased her back on the sofa, taking the gray shawl and putting it over her, then lay down beside her.

"To keep you safe, I made you a prisoner here," he murmured. "It worries me that you went out unaccompanied, though perhaps there was no harm in it. I wonder where the guards I set had gone to."

"I saw no one," she whispered. "What did they look like?"

"Oh, they could be my cousins," he replied. "Tall. Dark. Of course, they stood watch in shifts and were never there all at once. But each man was skilled at not being seen, so perhaps that was why you did not."

He vowed to get the reason from the three as soon as he returned to the house by St. James's Square. It seemed to him now that Todt had dodged him and the other two, Vladimir and Sasha, had not been there at all.

He would take their tails if they had been derelict in their duty, he thought with fury.

Angelica nestled closer. If all she had in the world was him, he would do his utmost to protect her. He shifted, feeling the ruff hairs on his back press against his shirt. She seemed to bring out the beast in him in so many ways. A guardian. A mate. Whatever she needed, he would be that. His mind wandered. Holding her near had that effect on him too.

"You seemed happy here," he said absently. "Why?"

She took a while to answer. "When you opened the door of this house, it was as if one life had ended and another began, Semyon."

Again she paused. He waited.

"After what happened, I thought I might have gone mad and—that I was imagining this—this peacefulness."

"I think I understand." But he knew he could not see it through her eyes. Still he listened.

"I was too afraid to run, but I thought to," she said honestly. "I could never repay your kindness. Nor did I believe you would want me for long."

"Did you think I was playing the hero by rescuing you?"

"Never. But it was—is—too strange to make sense of, Semyon."

"Indeed." He turned his head when he heard a scratching at the window.

"It is the cat, patting with its paw," she murmured. "In or out, it is never sure of what is best."

Just before he turned back to her, he caught a glimpse of something that was not a cat's paw, but much larger. It was a man's hand, blunt-fingered, callused, spread across the pane as if testing its strength.

He let her go and rose to the window, staring at nothing. Whoever the hand belonged to had vanished.

"Is it Puss? Shall we let her in?" She seemed completely unaware of the danger and he looked at her, deciding to keep it that way.

"There was a bird. She's jumped away."

"Then come back to me." She stretched out her arms.

Semyon enfolded her body with his own. "Yes, love. Then . . ."

She would not let him say. But he vowed silently to take her from this house and never return.

Chapter 9

Semyon had not told her of his reasons for bringing her to his family house near St. James's Square, but here she was. It was a strange place, larger inside than it seemed from the street, although he had hustled her so quickly from the same black carriage in which she'd been brought away from captivity that she had not seen many details.

He had warned her in no uncertain terms to stay indoors no matter what. She had been here for only a few days, in a chamber that seemed to be reserved for guests, if she was one. Angelica thought she had heard him berating someone for not guarding her, but she was not sure who.

Her chamber was a pleasant place, elegantly if sparely furnished, and situated on the top floor with something of a view, at least in winter. She could see the tops of leafless trees and through them, some of the Thames and both sides of its banks.

Today the sky was overcast with scudding clouds but at least there was no rain. There had been a steady downpour when she had gone from her first sanctuary to this one.

Semyon had insisted that she move by night, and had sent help, telling her that he could not be seen about the premises. A family advisor had counseled discretion, she gathered, without that person knowing the precise details of who she was or why she had been secreted away in the mews house in Mayfair.

She turned to the closed door, hearing a familiar tread upon the stairs. Semyon knocked lightly and entered.

"My dear Angelica—how nice to see you in my, ah, lair."

"Is it yours? I thought you said your rooms were elsewhere in this house."

"Yes, yes, they are and I shall take you there presently. Have you settled in?"

"Somewhat." She gestured to the enormous trunk. "I haven't unpacked. But then I never did pack, in the strict sense of the word, I mean. I just threw everything into that and pointed to it when those silent fellows came."

He nodded. "Of course. What else could you do?"

"Who were they, Semyon?"

"Your three invisible bodyguards," he said crossly. "Making them lift so much heavy stuff seemed like a suitable punishment for the time you gave them the slip."

"Oh dear." She felt sorry that they had been punished for her misdeed.

"Never mind that, Angelica." His gaze swept the room. "Do you have everything you think you might need? As we discussed, it is unwise for you to leave here for the present."

"Yes, I think so." She waved a hand at the shelves. "It was kind of you to provide so many books."

"Most were already here." He walked to the shelves and peered at the spines. "An interesting selection. Novels. Poetry. A fair number of bound treatises on science and anthropology and such—one of my kinsmen has just finished writing his own, on the history of our clan."

Angelica gave him an interested look. "I ought to read it. Have you?"

"Not yet. I am waiting for the reviews to come out, so I can pretend I have, though." He grinned. "I am afraid it might put you to sleep."

"I think you like me that way," she said impishly.

"You are particularly luscious *en déshabille* and you know it. Closed eyes and parted lips and your hair tumbling over a pillow—" He took a deep breath and controlled himself, turning back to the shelves. "Where was I in my inventory? You are far too distracting. Ah, yes." He scowled at the books as if they were the cause of his discomfort. "There is a set of encyclopedias and Dr. Johnson's excellent dictionary. Natural history. Travelogues."

She went to where he was and took out a volume from the shelf he was looking at. "Then I will not feel the urge to roam." She opened it and riffled the pages. "Ah. This one is about Canada. It seems that nine-tenths of the map is blank. What did the author find to write about?"

"Forests. Voyageurs. Beaver trappers."

She closed the book and put it back. "Do you know, I was thinking of escaping from London and traveling there by ship. Or to the American colonies."

"Whatever for?" he asked, astonished.

"I had no idea if the men who kidnapped me would return. It seemed wrong to expect a gallant stranger to risk his life for me a second time."

He gave her a wry smile. "Thank you. But I can't imagine you in a canoe. Or living in a cabin."

"Well, then you have saved me from those fates too," she laughed.

He put his arms around her and pressed a kiss to her forehead. "That is good to hear. Stay cheerful, Angelica. And now I must go."

She could not help but pout. His mouth came down over hers and he made it go away. She was breathless when he raised his head.

"I will come to you tonight," he said softly, caressing her cheek. "Your meals will arrive at the usual times. You might meet Natalya. She rules our kitchen. Or she might send someone up with a tray."

"Very well."

He heard the dismay in her voice. "For now it is best if you keep somewhat to yourself, my dear. There are also pencils and paper and pens and watercolors."

"I will paint you new wallpaper then." She nodded at the print on the walls. "That is rather busy. A flower, is it? How it repeats. And repeats. I shall be quite dizzy if I look at it too long."

"I am not sure. It is either a flower or a pawprint. Take your pick."

She squinted again at the walls. "A paw flower, perhaps."

"Ah, that is it! I believe it is a pawpaw blossom. It is tropical," he explained.

"Oh."

"Anyway, you will not grow dizzy from looking at it. Irritable, perhaps, but then you can always look at something else, my dear. You will be well provided for, and as I said, I will be up to visit you the moment I return."

"Is it a secret that I am in this house?"

"Not to those who matter. But there are a few who believe only those of our blood or those married to one of our clan should be allowed in. I must respect their opinions on the matter for now."

He pointed to the ceiling.

"What? Are they—up there?"

"No," he smiled. "I was about to say that there is another half-floor. We use it for a storeroom but there is a better view from there if you are restless. Almost a bird's-eye view in some spots, if you are not afraid of heights."

"No, I am not."

"Good. You can count every church steeple in London from there."

Angelica thought of the deconsecrated church she had gone into and wondered if she could see it too. The steeple would simply come to a point, of course, with no cross, so it was likely to stand out from the others for that reason alone.

She nodded. "And I am free to go up there, I suppose, or you would not tell me of it."

"Exactly. Keeping you confined is difficult. I thought I would give you permission before you disobeyed me."

She pushed at his chest, laughing at his comment. "Go then. I will amuse myself." She stretched up and stood on tiptoes to kiss him good-bye.

The hours passed swiftly. She found a novel that amused her for a while, then set it aside to finish the mending of her dress and chemise, a task she had set aside on that day of restlessness.

That done, she decided to go up to the storeroom before sunset and look about. She closed the door to her chamber behind her and headed up a twisting set of very narrow stairs in a niche by itself.

She pushed open the door at the top, expecting to be met by a musty smell, but the storeroom was airy, even bright, considering there were still clouds in the sky.

Angelica went to a window and kneeled beside it. It was possible for her to stand upright but the view was so lovely she wanted to enjoy it until the day faded away.

There to her left was the majestic white bulk of St. Paul's cathedral. The sun glowed on its colossal dome as if in blessing. It did seem as if she could see all the church steeples in London, poking up high and white above lower buildings, and to amuse herself, she counted them—ah, there was one without a cross.

Nearer than she had thought.

Angelica felt a small prickle of uneasiness. Why had it been so easy for her to confess to a stranger and so hard for her to admit it to Semyon?

What he did not know would not hurt him, she reasoned. She had been overly emotional on that day and utterly unsure of herself. Feeling trapped was something that made her behave somewhat irrationally at the best of times, and these were not the best of times.

Her heart skipped a beat when she saw his tousled head far below. Even from this distance she could see he was otherwise well groomed, his shirt and stock collar a flash of white against the sober cloth of his tailored coat. He walked swiftly to the east, as if off on some important errand.

Gradually Angelica became aware that he was being followed. A shorter man in a hat of nondescript brown and coat of the same dull color was keeping several steps behind him.

As the two men traversed the crooked streets, she often lost sight of one or both of them, but when they came out on newer, straight thoroughfares, she saw them again.

Her last glimpse of Semyon was going up the broad stairs of a distant building with an official look, all pillars and molding and marble. The man following him stopped in front of it and seemed to be waiting for him to come out.

Eventually he gave up. Perhaps she was imagining things. But it was winter and the days were short. The waning light soon cast the scene in shadows too dark to spy anything.

By the time he returned, she was reading by the brilliant light of a many-armed candelabra. Its candles were new, with white wicks that she lit from the candle end that an unseen servant brought up with her supper. She had not reached the door quickly enough to see who it was, being wrapped up in yet another novel, but she called a thank-you to the youth she glimpsed going back down the stairs a floor below. He had answered in a foreign tongue—was it Russian?

Semyon had said that his forebears were from there.

She had clung to the banister high above and listened to what seemed to be preparations for a party. If she'd heard aright, they were calling it a Howl.

Angelica went back into her room and put a slip of paper in the novel to mark her place.

She felt like a child being kept upstairs and it would not do to sulk . . . especially if that was Semyon taking the stairs two at a time.

It was. She saw his handsome, smiling face laughing up at her from the stairwell and he waved his coat, which he had taken off. It was less than a minute before he was at her side, somewhat out of breath.

He took her by the shoulders and kissed her passionately. His nose was cold, very cold, from being outside and, she supposed, running back from wherever he'd been. She was so happy to see him that she forgot to mention the man she'd thought might have followed him.

"So. Grisha said he brought you a tray. Is there anything left on it?"

"Fat little dumplings. Dark bread. Both very good and I ate

some of each. And there is a glass of very strong spirits which I did not touch."

"Piroshki! Vodka! Wonderful!" He headed straight for the leftovers and made short work of them, tossing the clear drink down his throat and pretending to breathe fire at her.

She waved the smell of alcohol away. "Ugh."

He only laughed. "We say it will put hair on your chest."

She came over and undid his collar and the top buttons of his shirt. "Yours seems to be more luxuriant already."

He glanced down. "How odd. So it does."

She made herself comfortable on his knee and they dallied pleasurably for a while. He began to murmur into her neck but not the sweet things she loved to hear. No, he was making an excuse to leave her once again.

"Oh no, Semyon. Where are you going now? It is so dark out."

"Three floors below," he said heartily. "It is a sort of party that we have once in a while. Men only, my dear. We call it a Howl."

"I thought I heard someone say that word."

"Then don't be surprised if you hear a few!" He growled like a wild thing and bit her neck excitingly hard in several places.

"Oh! Mmm! More!"

He rose with her in his arms and dropped her on the bed. "If that was a request for my amorous services, the answer is yes. But later. I am expected downstairs and I am already late."

"Fie, Semyon!"

He got on all fours over her and rolled her around with what felt like a paw to her, truly, growling and nipping and being so amusingly rowdy that she got out of breath from laughing.

Then he bounded and crossed the room in a few swift strides before she collected herself enough to stop him.

"I shall return," he intoned, "prepare to be ravished."

"Oh, all right." She waved a weak good-bye, still laughing, and let him go.

The tall new candles had burned low and he still had not returned. Angelica felt a little peevish. The noise from downstairs made it clear that the Howl was going strong.

Hmph. She was running out of patience. He might be in no condition to ravish her if he stayed there much longer, swilling that clear stuff.

She rose from the armchair where she'd passed the last hour or so and went to the door, opening it a crack.

There was no one in the hall.

She went to the stairs and looked down the spiraling well. No one was there either.

Angelica frowned. She set a slippered foot quietly upon the first step . . . and somehow all the rest, all the way down to the first floor, were quickly traversed.

The entire household had to be celebrating, for there was no one anywhere about but her.

The door to a high-ceiling hall was ajar and it was from there that the noise was coming.

She hesitated, not wanting to catch Semyon's eye or be seen by anyone, deciding to go back up a few steps and crane her neck for a peek.

The assembled company let loose all of a sudden in a hugely resonant, multivoiced howl.

The sound was thrilling, reverberating in the stairwell and all through the house. They howled again. Angelica put her hands over her ears and hoped they would not be at it all night long.

But the enormous sound died down and the ordinary ruckus of a drunken party resumed.

She stepped backward and up one more time and then she peeked.

Angelica gasped.

There were men about the table inside the hall and . . . not-men.

She knew no word that would describe those beings.

All were dressed in good English clothes: immaculate linen shirts and stock collars, undone in the warmth of the room, coats flung over chairs or the nearest friend. But the ones who amazed her had . . . fur.

Luxurious fur, combed back and away from their necks and heads. Their well-groomed paws were as large as the hands of strong men, with dark, tapered nails. They looked like wolves, she thought wonderingly.

As if to prove her right, all of them threw their heads back and howled at the same time.

The wild sound echoed until she felt she would go mad from hearing it.

They did it again.

This time she looked into the mouths of the ones who seemed truly men and saw fangs of such length and wickedness that she felt faint. And extraordinarily long tongues.

Angelica blushed.

Semyon had such a tongue. And thinking of where it had been made her blush turn hotter.

But he had been in every way a man, she thought with shock. She'd had her hands all over him, kissed him, looked over every inch of his nakedness—he was most definitely a man and nothing else.

Her heart sank.

Where was he now? She had not seen him at the table. If his back was to her, she would still recognize him.

Angelica stood upon the stair, clinging to the banister, feeling a wave of vertigo. She heard chairs inside the room scrape upon the floor and the awkward sounds of bodies rising clumsily.

Toasts were proposed, healths were drunk. In English. In Russian.

She dared not move.

Angelica went backward up the stairs but she faced forward.

If a wolf . . . or wolf man . . . were to pounce upon her, she wanted to see his face.

Step by step. Up. Back.

And what if, she asked herself, *what if that wolf man were Semyon Taruskin?*

The monster who had kidnapped her from the house of the Congreves seemed quite ordinary by comparison. Recognizably human.

She reminded herself that Semyon had never hurt her in the slightest, had vowed not to, and had shown himself to be loyal in the highest degree.

Fangs. Fur. Paws. Did he have—could he be—had she seen— No, he had none of those attributes.

A knock on the outer door made her retreat into the shadows. Whoever it was knocked again and she saw an older man, who seemed human in every detail of his person, cross the marble floor to answer it.

Outside stood a man, bundled against the cold, who spoke to him in a quiet voice. She strained to hear over the continuing hubbub of the party in the high-ceilinged hall.

There was something familiar about his stocky build, even about his low voice.

It hit her like a thunderbolt: he was the man who had given her the poisoned rose. The man she had taken for a guest of the Congreves, another who, like Semyon, had lost his way.

Transfixed, she watched as he handed a *carte de visite* to the older man who answered the door, but she could not hear to whom he wanted it given.

That done, he muttered a good night and the older man closed the door. He glanced at the card he'd been given and set it on a silver tray on a sideboard in the foyer.

He went into the hall and she heard raucous cries from around the table that ran to one thing. "Ivan! Come and drink with us!"

Evidently he'd refused, because he came back out again with . . . Semyon.

She held her breath and her heart banged against her ribs. Angelica scarcely dared to look at him, but he seemed at first glance like a man.

Her eyes ran frantically over his tall figure, seeing nothing out of the ordinary. The hair on his head was shaggier than usual, perhaps. And—she peered through the shadows where she hid—his barber needed to carefully shave his neck in back, because it had grown rather thick—

Angelica pressed a hand firmly over her heart lest it burst through her flesh.

He was one of them. He had to be.

The sound of his low voice speaking to Ivan stilled her all the same. It was as soothing as it had been coming from the pillow next to hers, as good humored as it had been over breakfast.

"Who brought this?"

"He did not say his name," Ivan replied.

"Did you ask him, Ivan?"

"Yes, of course." The older man seemed faintly offended. "He shook his head and said just to give you that card."

"But there is nothing engraved on it." Semyon turned it over in his fingers. "Ah. Now I see."

"He wrote those initials. S.S."

Semyon gave a frustrated sigh. "Did he say anything else?"

"That you were to meet that gentleman—not him, that S.S.—at St. Paul's. Under the dome. In the very center."

"How strange," Semyon said thoughtfully. "But it is a public place. I suppose I will be safe enough."

She wanted to run to him, but she was rooted to the spot. Angelica hated the idea of listening at doors and yet she had done just that. The person named Ivan seemed very much in charge around this house, and yet not someone with authority over Semyon.

Certainly Ivan was someone who was not supposed to know about her, or someone she was supposed to keep her distance from.

Semyon flicked the card in Ivan's direction and the older man caught it in midair. "You're going?"

"Yes, why not?"

Ivan shook his head slowly. "What shall I tell the others?"

"If I am not back in an hour and a half, tell them to come get me," Semyon said airily. "One for all and all for all. Wait a minute. Did I get that right, Ivan?"

Angelica realized he'd had a lot to drink.

"I don't know, sir," the older man said tightly. "I don't read tales of derring-do."

Semyon chucked him under the chin, to Ivan's enormous irritation. "You worry too much. Off I go, then."

"Do you even know who the person is?"

"I have an idea."

"Who, then?"

The exact question she would have put to him herself.

"St. Sin, I think. Who else could it be?"

Ivan could make no sense of the name and shook his head in a baffled way as he closed the door behind Semyon.

He returned the way he had come, taking no notice of Angelica. She turned around and dashed upstairs.

Chapter 10

Semyon entered the immense cavern that was St. Paul's through a side door, having bribed a brass polisher who was working late.

The coins were valuable enough to make the man head for the nearest pub and drink up at least one sovereign. Semyon stepped over the rag smeared with polish and the little jar that held the stuff as he moved inside the cathedral.

He was glad for the chance to look around.

The vast, shadowy dome seemed to float overhead, its grandeur barely visible, even with the moonlight coming through the small round windows in it.

Semyon walked quietly, more on the sides of his leather boots than the harder heels. The large black-and-white tiles matched the stride of a tall man. He kept to the outer edge of the circular floor directly under the dome, unwilling to strike out for the center on the black pathways leading to it.

There was no one there, anyway.

He paused to listen for . . . he knew not what. Or who.

A wandering deacon? A man with a mop?

Even this magnificent edifice, the pride of London, needed mopping.

He heard nothing for some minutes.

And then a shadow detached itself from one of the high recesses behind the square pillars that seemed to support the grand dome.

A man. With a stocky, compact build and measured tread.

Semyon stayed where he was, instinctively sniffing to see if he could pick up a scent.

Beneath the churchly smells of hymnals and pious exhalations there was something different.

It was a faint smell of decay. Like bad teeth. Or something worse.

Semyon, already on his guard, stiffened. That smell alone proved the connection of the kidnapper's lair to St. Sin.

But would he meet that notorious individual or only this fellow?

The stocky man walked to the very center of the floor under the dome. He looked up to the gallery high above that ran round its gigantic circumference.

Then he looked straight ahead at nothing.

"Come, Mr. Taruskin," he said clearly. "Follow me."

Semyon drew in a silent breath and hesitated. He could be shot if he revealed himself. It seemed incredible to him that such a thing could happen in this holy place, but he dared not put his trust in men.

Still—if it meant meeting whoever had engineered the kidnapping of Angelica, he would do it.

He wanted that man, or men, to know that he would tear their throats if they did not leave her alone. Semyon had no idea how they had figured out where he lived, but he remembered, with a flash of chagrin, Ivan's scolding over his lack of discretion.

He had only himself to blame.

The stocky man walked out of the center to another recess, singing tunelessly under his breath. The grating, unpleasant sound echoed in the half-domes of all the recesses, then, faintly and finally at the top of the great dome that surpassed them all.

Semyon saw that he was walking to the staircase that led to the gallery around the dome's circumference.

Up he went, tedious step by tedious step, wheezing now and no longer singing. Semyon had no choice but to follow him—there was only one way up.

When the stocky man set foot on the gallery floor at last, Semyon had nearly caught up to him.

"Sit there," the man said, pointing.

Semyon stayed standing. At least he was near a route of escape. That was something.

"You must sit. And turn your ear to the wall," the other man said over his shoulder.

Semyon understood. He would hear St. Sin, but not see him. No doubt the mysterious Sin would sit exactly halfway from where he was, knowing that his words would run around the dark dome, quite clear in the silence.

Semyon listened to the stocky man's footsteps go on and then stop. He sat down, doing as he'd been instructed.

He leaned his shaggy head back against the tiled wall, feeling quite sober. His head ached, though.

The solemn intonation of the disembodied voice in his ear startled him and his head cracked against the tiles.

Christ. Now it really ached.

"Good evening, Mr. Taruskin."

"What do you want? And who are you?"

The solemn voice laughed deeply. "I am St. Sin. You know who I am."

Semyon wanted to race around and crack the fellow's head

against his side of the tiled dome. "How do you know that I know?"

There was no more laughter, just silence for a long moment. "Because you sent a man to poke around where he was not wanted. I heard that he was investigating and had him followed. So many interesting roads lead to the house of the Pack of St. James."

Semyon would not answer.

"Never mind. I expect His Majesty will protect you all."

Semyon held his breath. The connection between the court and his kinsmen was an old one but the secret had never been made public.

"What do you want?" he asked again.

"The beauty in your keeping, of course." The low voice held more than a trace of ill-concealed lust. "Angelica Harrow."

"Leave her alone."

There was a pause. "You can give her to me or I will have her taken."

Semyon stood up and roared into the shadows. "Go to hell, Sin!"

The booming laugh he got in reply took a long time to die down. Semyon grabbed the railing, unable to believe that he and the owner of the disembodied voice and the stocky man were the only people in the enormous edifice.

He strained his eyes to see and waited for a minute, then another for his wolf-sight to come to him.

Everything brightened when it did. As clearly as if the sun was rising over the high altar he saw a heap of bodies near it. Were they dead? No . . . they were breathing. Barely. No doubt drugged somehow, just as Angelica had been drugged.

The thought that he was being jerked about like a dog on a chain by someone he could not even see infuriated him. The danger to Angelica made his ruff rise and his face turn to full fur. He willed the change to happen faster. He could feel his clothes splitting at the seams and he dropped to all fours.

On noiseless paws he ran along the railing to where he had last heard the voice speak, his angry blood roaring in his pricked ears.

He was too late.

The mastermind of Angelica's kidnapping and his stocky henchman had anticipated his change. Even provoked it. Panting, Semyon came in wolf form to the opposite side. A ladder of rope and wood was fastened to the railing, swaying, creaking.

Two men were walking over the black-and-white tiles of the central floor. The stocky one opened one of the great doors to the outside, and waved a very tall man through it.

Semyon could not change back quickly enough. His paws would not wrap around rope and he did not dare make the terrifyingly high leap from where he was to the floor. If he broke a bone in wolf form, he would remain that way until it was fully healed.

The great door closed behind the men. His golden eyes glared in the darkness they left behind them.

Chapter 11

Frantic with worry, Angelica retreated to her chamber. She knew she could not spy upon Semyon from above—it was too dark and the streets were sunk in deep shadows. But she went to the window all the same.

Here and there a pool of light from one of the new gas lamps illuminated a corner, and she caught a glimpse of a hurrying figure. It was a watchman. She could hear his distant cry of the hour.

She withdrew and sank upon the bed, marveling again at what she had seen in the great hall below.

The strange creatures had the air of gentlemen, for all their fur and claws and fangs. She had never heard of anything like them and had not imagined wolf men could exist. She was thankful that Semyon seemed to share only some of their traits—but how would she confront him when he returned?

He had done everything for her and saved her from a terrible fate. All he had asked in return was for her to stay in the second sanctuary he had provided for her, in his home and the home of his kinsmen.

She rose and looked at herself in the mirror for a long moment, wondering if the magical transformation of human to animal was happening to her as well. Perhaps simply being within the walls of this strange house could cause it.

No. She was the same. She ran her hands over her smooth cheeks and neck, feeling only softness, then lifted up her hair to see if her nape was smooth as well, twisting for a better look.

It was. She set her hands upon the top of the chest of drawers and looked deep into her own eyes, searching for the piercing wildness she had seen in Semyon's.

Now she remembered him watching from the street and how yellow his eyes had seemed even from that distance. She had thought then that he looked wild and watchful as a wolf, but her disordered state of mind and the terror of her captivity had made her think all sorts of things.

So. Her own eyes looked much the same. But they were luminous with fear and wonder.

Not fear of him. But of what the future might bring.

Her heart was pounding and blood surged in her veins. Angelica felt hot all over, and rubbed nervously at her clothes, trying to subdue a sudden itch.

Dear God. Would she begin to come out in fur like the revelers below? She would tear it out of her skin if she did.

Angelica unfastened her gown and the draped undergarment beneath, baring herself to her own gaze.

Her breasts heaved from her panicked breathing but they proved to be as smooth and hairless as her face and neck. She ran her hands over herself everywhere, reaching and turning—

"Now that is a pretty sight." Semyon's low voice made her start and grab the chest of drawers for support as she turned her face to him.

He stood in the doorway, looking disheveled and out of breath himself.

"You!" Her gasp subsided as her gaze ran over him. She perceived no real difference in him.

He looked, in fact, like a gentleman who'd had a convivial night and gone out for a bracing walk in the cold to revive himself.

He smiled at her.

Angelica's foolish heart wanted to melt. She let go and turned fully to him, drawing together the folds of her gown and concealing her nakedness.

"What were you doing, my dear? Admiring your own beauty?"

"I thought I might have—a flea on my person. I felt a bite and . . ." She trailed off.

"I will speak to the housemaster immediately," he laughed. "Although I must say, I cannot blame the flea for wanting a taste of such sweet flesh. But herbs can be strewn and powders applied to the carpets, just in case."

He came all the way into the room and closed the door behind him. She shrank back as he put his hand over hers and gently tried to separate the folds she was clutching. "May I see?"

"N-no," she replied, moving his hand away. What if he turned into a full beast, like the ones she had seen in the hall below. Would he allow her to refuse him then?

Or would he simply pounce?

"Not now, Semyon," she managed to say. "There is a—a chill in the room."

"Let me warm you," he said seductively.

She backed away. "Please. I am not in an amorous mood."

He studied her for a long moment. "A pity. Forgive me, then. But the sight of you caressing yourself so avidly made me forget all else."

She composed herself. "Did you enjoy yourself at the gathering of your clan? I—I did not expect it to last so long."

She would not tell him that she'd peeked through the door or what she'd seen. Or that she knew he had left the house, summoned by the mysterious man known as St. Sin.

He had not been gone that long. What had happened at the great cathedral?

She suspected he would never tell her. Angelica sat down on the bed, twisting her hands together and not looking at him.

"Forgive me also for leaving you alone for so long." His fingers slipped under her chin and tilted her face to his.

She stared into his eyes, seeing only the hazel color she knew and not piercing yellow. Their warmth suffused her and melted the inner fear she struggled to conceal.

"You have seen something tonight," he said quietly, searching her eyes more intently than she'd done his. "What was it?"

"Nothing."

He let go and straightened, going to the window. "This room is too high up for anyone to look in. And the walls cannot be scaled by intruders."

"I saw nothing out the window once the sun went down but the reflection of this room."

He clasped his hands behind his back and stood strongly with his legs apart, the picture of a dominant, watchful male.

"And did you stay inside it, Angelica?"

"Of course."

"I would like to believe you."

She made a nervous gesture, as if warding him off.

"If these windows were magic, they would show the reflections of all the hours since I left you here. I would know if you opened the door and left. And they would show the face of the clock and I would know exactly when you went. And when you returned."

She trembled. "Are they magic?"

"No. Only glass. They reflect the present moment and that is all."

His calm tone made her extremely uneasy.

"But there is magic in this house, Semyon. You did not tell me of it when you brought me here."

"One thing at a time." His low voice was close to a growl and she shuddered to hear it. "You left this room, didn't you, Angelica?"

She nodded, summoning up all her courage to tell him the truth.

"I was so lonely that I went downstairs," she began, forcing her voice to remain steady. "The door to the great hall was ajar and I—I looked."

"So now you know. We are a brotherhood of wolf men."

She swallowed hard. "You seem more human than some of the others."

"Sometimes. It is a difficult trait to control." He began to pace in slow strides.

She could not help but look at him, taking in every particular to see if he was Semyon the man and not Semyon the wolf.

Angelica verified that his physical aspects were fully human. That left something she could not see: his soul.

"Who are you, Semyon?" she whispered desperately.

"I will tell you." He took a small book down from a shelf that was too high for her to reach, a book she had not seen until this minute. He sat by her.

Penned by a long-ago scribe in a strange and unfamiliar alphabet, the text was illuminated by beautifully colored miniature paintings in an ancient style. He read from it but it seemed to her that he did not speak. It was as if the words flowed from his mind to hers.

Born under the blue sun that never sets, the great ice wolves of the north ran before the never-ending winds. In time their wild blood mingled with the men of a warrior clan, the legendary heroes known as Roemi . . .

When he had told the tale and explained some of the powers he possessed, she made him stop. Bravely she put a hand upon his arm.

"I understand, Semyon," was all she said. "And I love you as you are."

He closed the old book and turned to her. "Good. You and I must be as one now and not only in bed. There are some among the Pack who protest your presence here—and others in the ordinary world who would harm you. I had a message from the man known as St. Sin and tried to meet him tonight, but he kept himself invisible."

"From you?"

Semyon made a wry face. "I can be fooled. He was on the opposite side of the gallery under the dome of St. Paul's cathedral."

"I know it. I wandered there once to hear evensong."

"Did you climb to the gallery?"

"No."

"It is a gigantic circle with a railing. Had I run round, St. Sin would have matched me stride for stride, always staying ahead."

"Then how—"

"It is a whispering gallery, a marvel of its size. Words spoken on the other side travel to the ear as if the speaker were standing next to the hearer. Sin took full advantage of it."

"Did another man not come for you?"

"Yes. That was Hinch, but he is only an underling."

"He was the man who gave me the poisoned rose. And I think he carried me away somehow from the Congreves' house to the place where you found me."

"Then you saw him at the door tonight."

She nodded fearfully. "I almost thought to follow you out, but I was frightened of him."

"Hmm. It is good that you stayed behind for once. I suppose you are capable of obeying after all."

"Now and then," she said, a note of ruefulness in her soft voice.

"Ah, Angelica. You may be the death of me, but I do not mind."

She turned to him and twined her arms around his neck, knowing that her undone gown fell open again and not caring.

He blew the candles out and they made love by moonlight. Silent, unhurried love, deep and true.

Chapter 12

"Stage another kidnapping? We dare not even try. Have you gone mad?"

"Of course I am. I find that it pays."

The man who had spoken first, the younger of the two sitting at a rickety table, looked defiantly at his business partner, then nodded at the whiskey bottle between them. "*That* only makes the madness worse."

"I don't care. I must have my drop." The older man smiled in a nasty way.

"Hah. No such thing where you are concerned. You could drink a distillery dry."

St. Sin only laughed. "Have a drop yourself, Victor. And don't argue with me." He pulled the cork out of the bottle and poured the amber liquid within it into a large glass, upending the bottle over it. "Oh dear. There is none left. I shall send you out for more."

"Send Hinch."

Sin frowned. "He is dead to the world at the moment."

"Already drunk?"

"That is his business if he is, Victor. You have become as prim as a parson."

"One of us ought to have his wits about him."

Sin clicked his fingernail against the glass before he drank again. "Indeed. So far you have not."

"What do you mean, sir?"

"You know exactly what I am talking about—the beauty you pledged for sale. Angelica is a valuable commodity and you made a hash of her abduction from start to finish."

"Let her go," Victor Broadnax stated emphatically. "You know where she is and who she is with. We cannot risk it."

Sin waved the glass at him. "It would be fun to steal her under from under Semyon Taruskin's nose."

"He would kill to defend her, I think."

The older man shrugged indifferently. "He cannot be everywhere at once. Did I tell you that I inveigled him into St. Paul's cathedral for a chat?"

Vicotr looked surprised. "No. When did you do that?"

"Two nights ago. What he would not tell me, I guessed. It was great fun to provoke him. I tell you, Victor, he is not at all what he seems." He held back from telling him of Semyon's transformation, hating to tip his hand.

"But that is a very public place, where the devout go to pray."

Sin smiled widely. "Yes. Hinch handed out hymnbooks dusted with sleeping poison to them and helpfully pointed out the page for vespers. He gave small bribes to the few others about. We soon had a barely breathing heap of the first and the bribed ones vanished as requested."

"Hmm. I am not a religious man. But God may strike you down yet."

Sin shot him a contemptuous look. "But I consider myself in his service."

"You are quite mad," Victor said again, looking at the door

and wondering if he should make a dash for it and leave his partner to rake in his ill-gotten money.

He decided against it for now. Until he could figure out a way to find the money, which was hidden, and steal it. Send old Sin swimming in the Thames into the bargain. Imagining the gray water closing over his partner's head was comforting.

"Am I? I suspect the quality may run in your family. Angelica is a free spirit, if you prefer that term, and seems impossible to control. You said as much when you first told me of her upbringing."

Victor traced a crack in the tabletop with his finger, not looking at his partner. "Not as free as that. We all must eat. She managed to survive on her own for three years in London without going on the town or being kept. Apparently she would rather work."

"Unlike you." Sin could not resist the jab. He took a swig from the glass and smacked his lips. "We are operating at a loss half the time."

"Is that my fault? The orgies you host are expensive."

"Of course they are. We cater to the upper class and the peerage. Noblemen do not want to squirm about on a dirty floor with strumpets."

"I am not so sure of that," Victor muttered. "Men will take their pleasure anywhere, it seems, noble or not."

Sin scowled at him, mutely conceding the point. "Ah, but it is the women that we want." He drank the entire contents of the glass in one go, his unshaven gorge working noisily. But he didn't cough and his eyes weren't watering when he set down the glass. His stare was a cold, unblinking blue. "Allow me to instruct you on the subject of wealthy, dissolute females. One. Mere pleasure bores them."

Victor gave him a disgusted look. "Two. They enjoy humiliating others and being humiliated themselves."

"You *have* been listening."

"But tell me again, Sin. Just in case I missed anything."

The other man stood up, towering over him. He had once been handsome and his features still had a chiseled look. But the ravages of drink and disease showed in his face—and his cruelty showed in his eyes. "Three. Certain women relish unimaginable wickedness and one must be very creative to satisfy them."

"Yes, yes. So you have said. And bragged."

"Should I not brag? My best customers want an iron-willed man who is not afraid to give them what they secretly crave. Proper punishment can be highly stimulating when administered with a firm hand. You are too young and callow to be convincing at that game."

Victor rubbed a hand over his cheek, which was soft and peachlike, compared to Sin's furrowed lines and scars. "Perhaps I should stick to the virgins then."

The older man scowled. "Which brings us back to your sister. You were a fool to take the shackle off her ankle," he said contemptuously.

"She was supposed to be delivered to her purchaser in flawless condition. And she is my stepsister, if you have forgotten that fact."

Sin seemed unimpressed. "Ah, yes. But that is to our advantage. No sentimental connection whatsoever once everyone who would care about her was dead, eh?"

"I don't think anyone much cared for her alive," Victor replied. "It bred a toughness in her. It is hard to see unless you know her well, but it is there."

"Whatever you say. I expect you swindled her out of whatever pittance she inherited. In fact, I am sure you did."

Victor only shrugged.

"Thought so," Sin said with malicious satisfaction.

"Shut up." Victor rose, assuming a threatening stance that looked absurd next to his partner in crime. Despite being twenty years older, Sin was still powerfully built and physically imposing.

"And," Sin went on, "now that we know where she is, thanks to Hinch's skulking about in Mayfair and elsewhere and my ruse to entice him out of his lair—"

"Is there nothing you do not congratulate yourself for?"

Sin waved the comment away. "It ought to be easy enough to waylay her near St. James's Square."

"Not if she is under Semyon Taruskin's protection. From what little you have told of him—"

"The girl does as she pleases when he is not looking. She goes out in disguise. She talks to strangers. How fortunate that I was one."

"I cannot believe that she confessed to you as you said! Did you not guess that it was Angelica?"

"Not until she began to speak. She was completely veiled in gray and I watched her for a while. I thought she was a friend of the marquise, who went first."

"Devout also, I suppose."

Sin nodded. "In her way, yes. That lovely lady confesses to things that scorch my ears and demands that I impose an exciting penance. Whipping her soft arse, for one. She begs to have it done, again and again."

"Then and there?" Victor asked with disgust.

"Of course not. We meet later in her home, behind closed doors. There is only so much one can get away with in public."

"What did you tell Angelica?"

"Nothing. I muttered some nonsense to her after she poured out her heart to me. She seemed to be grateful, so it is true, you see, that I am of service to troubled souls. Would you like to know what she said about you?"

"No." Victor sat heavily in his chair again.

"I had thought you were lying about her innocence, Victor. Apparently not."

"However did she hang on to that after three years in London?" he muttered. "Unguarded and alone, working for her bread and butter, living hand to mouth."

The older man grunted. "Not any more. She has been with Semyon for days now. The man is rich. And he is a rake."

"And, from what you have told of him so far, he is also dangerous. And so are his brothers. What else do you know? I have heard some strange things whispered about the house in St. James's Square."

The other man's cold eyes grew colder. "The Taruskins are descended from strange blood, that is why."

"What do you mean?"

Sin scowled. "Their clan serves the king in secret. No man knows exactly how, and it is a hanging offense to speak of it."

"A pity." Victor would not mind seeing Sin swung by his neck. It would save him the trouble of drowning him.

But Sin continued to talk, made bold by the whiskey warming his guts. "I was fucking a wicked little duchess who longed most avidly to have the eldest, Kyril, in her bed. With an iron collar around his strong neck, of course. She offered me thousands of pounds to ensnare him."

"And?" Victor was suddenly curious.

"I could not. He had no hidden flaw that I could exploit, unlike that cousin of his—Lukian, yes, that was his name. The mightiest of them all, but his soul was consumed by his weakness for morphine. He died of it, I think. Or not. Anyway, he is dead. The others seem to possess a preternatural vitality. And unusual—abilities—that are almost magical."

"Do you mean illusions? Smoke and mirrors and other tricks of the stage?"

"No," Sin said flatly. "I would know."

"Of course. You were an actor. What was your greatest role again? As I remember, that story is not half-bad," Victor said in a sour voice. A new way to make money had occurred to him but he would need Sin's help. He would humor him, at least until he could kill him. The man could be grotesquely sentimental when he was drunk and it was amusing in a pathetic way.

Sin spoke to an imaginary balcony, his voice loud and raw from the whiskey. "I was playing a man of the cloth in—devil take it!" He paused, confused. "The name of the play escapes me. It was long ago. I was young then, younger than you are now."

"Go on." Victor stifled a yawn, irritated by Sin's declamatory tone.

"Anyway, I was supposed to be goodness itself, corrupted by a whore. Sally Gibbons had the role—I believe she married a duke eventually. She confessed her transgressions in lurid detail for a hundred and thirteen performances, night after night."

"And?"

"To cleanse her soul, I was required to scourge her. An illusion, of course, but the crowd loved it. I whipped the clothes off her to wild applause."

"For her acting, I hope."

Sin shook his head. "That was execrable. No. For her bared breasts, which were quite real. She got many curtain calls."

Victor could tell the story himself. "But you did not."

"Mine came later, after the show was over," Sin said with perverse pride. "I would be approached by a footman near the stage door when I left." He mimicked a servile tone. "Sir, milady wishes to speak to you privately. Please come this way to her carriage." He laughed, sending a whiskey smell into the air. "So I went. The first milady paid me handsomely to absolve her shocking tendency to vice and invent thrilling punishments that were even worse."

"Was she pretty?" Victor asked idly.

"Quite."

"What did you do to her?"

"Whatever she wanted. In the end her husband found out."

Victor nodded. He actually did not know the rest of the story.

"So," Sin went on, "I signed on for a repertory tour of the provinces to avoid his understandable wrath. I had hoped he might want to join in the fun, but no."

Victor gave a short laugh without much humor in it. "No one can leave town faster than an actor. Between your unpaid bills and the husbands you cuckolded, it is a wonder you are alive."

Sin had gone to a cabinet propped against the wall, ransacking it for more whiskey, finding a smaller bottle than the first. He slammed the top door and a lump of plaster fell to the floor.

"Tell me again why our headquarters must be in such a squalid place, if you are making so much money," Victor said.

"I like squalor. It reminds me of my humble beginnings," Sin replied.

"Why can we not move in to the house in the new area?"

"Too conspicuous. It is for our clients, not us," Sin said.

"Then allow me to rent one of the others. I wouldn't call myself notorious yet. Do you not hold all the leases and own the land beneath?"

Sin gave him a narrow look. "As a gift from my naughty marquise. There are some strings attached. Have you been busy looking up deeds and titles? I thought the Pack's secretary was doing that, the slight man with the spectacles. Antosha—that is his name. Hinch followed him."

Victor drummed his fingers on the table. "No, I heard you talking to Hinch when you were in your cups. Tell me, Sin, do you have a man follow me?"

"No," his business partner said blandly. "I was only asking. Let us think no more of that. Back to the matter of Angelica, if you please."

Chapter 13

The letter had come with the morning post. It had lain in the silver tray in the foyer with other missives, unnoticed, until Antosha had noticed the flamboyant style of the penmanship and that it was addressed to Semyon. He had turned it over to look at the wax seal.

He had invited the youngest of the Taruskin brothers into his study to give it to him and discuss it, if Semyon wished to, firmly shutting and locking the door behind him.

Now he looked on as Semyon slid a narrow blade under the seal. Antosha noted again the double initial impressed within the splotch of wax—S.S.—before the blade split them apart.

"Not like him," Semyon said, "to send an ordinary letter. I was expecting something more dramatic."

"Why?"

Semyon told the secretary about the sinister, echoing conversation in the whispering gallery. He'd hoped to keep quiet about it and not bring the censure of his kinsmen upon himself, but he did feel he could confide in Antosha. They seemed to have an understanding that went beyond Pack politics.

"St. Sin was once an actor, you know."

"Ah. That fits," Semyon said. "And how did you find that out?" He extracted two folded sheets of paper from the envelope but didn't read them.

"One subject leads to another," the secretary said, "and people like to talk. It seems that our adversary moves in the highest circles, though he is lowborn."

"A neat trick."

"He is good at them. And at playing both ends against the middle. Throw in a love of vice, a complete lack of conscience, and a talent for cheap theatrics, and that sums him up." Antosha pursed his lips and took out a leather-bound book. "If I share what I have found out, will you let me read that letter?"

"Of course."

He put his spectacles on and ran his finger down a list of names before he read them out. Semyon's eyes widened.

"There you have it," the secretary concluded. "St. Sin can be connected to many powerful people from ministers to great lords. He knows their secrets and they are in his debt."

"What sort of secrets?"

"Sexual ones."

"London is swarming with prostitutes of both sexes and there is plenty of work for all," Semyon said cynically as he sat back in his chair. "I do not understand why he would bother to kidnap Angelica."

Antosha shook his head. "Prostitutes are one thing and a genuine innocent is another. Angelica caught his eye somehow—or her stepbrother offered her up. That matters less than what will happen next."

Semyon bristled.

"Calm yourself. I am only pointing out that she must have

seemed like easy prey to both men before you happened along."

"Antosha!"

The secretary gave him a mild look. "Well, she is a beauty—yes, Semyon, I glimpsed her despite your precautions and I am not the only one in this house who has."

Semyon frowned but did not interrupt the rest of what the secretary wanted to say.

"At the moment, she is safe within our walls." He tapped at the names written in his book. "But she was meant for someone on this list. It would be interesting to find out who."

"If I tear out Sin's throat, it won't matter," Semyon growled.

Antosha peered at him. "Your fur is showing. Do you know, I think it appears when your emotions are violently stirred."

Semyon just glared at him.

"Anyway, if St. Sin has promised Angelica to a powerful man, he must make good on that promise."

"You speak as if you know these people."

"I know how they think. St. Sin has spun a web that has begun to entangle him as well. If he disappoints a client, then there will be retribution. And there are other things to worry about."

Semyon blew out a breath but it did little to relieve his anger. "Such as?"

"Sin is a heavy drinker and it has begun to unhinge his mind."

"Can we use that against him?"

Antosha smiled sadly. "We could, I suppose."

"Well, then—" Semyon began, leaning forward, the light of battle in his eyes.

"He is dangerously unpredictable. And the worst of it is that we do not know how much he knows about us."

Semyon fell silent.

"Certain missions may be compromised, you see," Antosha said. "The matter must be contained."

"I knew nothing of this."

"Your elder brothers preferred that you not know."

"Antosha, our secret work on behalf of the crown goes back centuries. Our wolfcraft enabled us to elude every spy there ever was."

"The Pack did maul a few now and then. Most undiplomatic."

Semyon disregarded that comment. "Sin is not a spy, is he?"

"No. But his degree of influence and his unscrupulousness would be very useful to the enemies of England. It is only a matter of time before someone makes good use of him."

Semyon thought for a minute. "The king and his innermost circle will not allow the government to be brought down by a flesh peddler."

"It has happened before." Antosha tapped the book again. "It can happen again. And we of the Pack will be brought down with it. Even exiled, perhaps."

A brooding silence filled the room and a sudden, icy rain began, spattering the windowpanes and freezing them over.

"I will not hand over Angelica to this monster," Semyon said in a very low voice.

"Good God, man. No one is asking you to do that," Antosha explained patiently. "But I think it would be best if she went to some other place just as safe for now. Somewhere not so near to the king's court. Until St. Sin loses interest and moves on to something else. Or dies of drink and dissipation, if we are lucky," he added.

"France? Holland?" Semyon asked desperately. "Where would I take her?"

"Not abroad. Sin can ask for a watch on outbound ships and he will get it. She would be arrested on some trumped-up charge and we would have a devil of a time getting her back. I would recommend the countryside. Heraldshire, perhaps. On the coast."

"Why there?"

"It has no forests and the surrounding fields are flat. The folk there are closemouthed and suspicious, and even a solitary visitor from elsewhere would be noticed."

"Would they welcome us?"

Antosha winked. "Money always helps. No one there will refuse it. They will hide her until you come for her again."

"I will not leave her, Antosha," Semyon said. "The Pack will have to do without me, and you will have to explain everything to Kyril and Marko and Ivan."

"I am getting that idea. By the way, the local smugglers dug tunnels to the sea cliffs. An escape can be made easily if necessary."

"Hmm." Semyon did not know what to do.

"Or she can stay here in London, if you leave a trail of clues heading out for Sin and his men to follow."

"I will talk to her," Semyon said.

Antosha gave him a quizzical look.

"She likes to decide for herself. And I do not care if wicked noblemen and corrupt ministers end up on the gallows with St. Sin."

"I see," Antosha said. "What about the Pack?"

"We will survive. We always have."

"And his majesty?"

"Long live the king," Semyon said dryly.

Antosha cleared his throat. "I had no idea you could be such a fool over a woman."

"She is no ordinary woman."

"I wish you both well. So," he nodded at the sheets of folded paper that Semyon was still holding. "What does the letter say?"

Semyon gave a slight start. "I forgot it was in my hand."

Antosha nodded as he began reading. A grimace of disgust and anger spread across his face. "He describes exactly what he will do to Angelica and to me when the time is come. It is all twisted filth." He crumpled the pages and rose to throw them into the fire.

They caught quickly and a thin smoke rose from them, filling the room. Antosha and Semyon were overcome by the time an intruder lifted the window. He and a stronger man dragged them out in seconds and into a waiting cart.

Angelica heard a commotion from her chamber on the topmost floor but did not dare to run downstairs.

Still, the nature of it and the names she heard—Semyon, Antosha—were enough to make her listen and creep closer.

Had the household forgotten her very existence? She reminded herself that not everyone knew of her presence there.

It seemed to her that something had happened to her man. There was shouting in the hall—she thought it was Ivan.

Carefully, noiselessly, she managed to go down another flight without being discovered.

Little by little some phrases made sense. But understanding them filled her with a nameless dread.

The front parlor window had been broken. Semyon and Antosha dragged out, bleeding. A noxious smoke had left two more men unconscious.

There was no doubt in her mind that her lover and the Pack's secretary had been taken against their will and she could easily guess the reason.

It had to be because of her. Angelica could not face the Pack, not knowing where she stood with any of them and fearing the worst. They had two more injured to see to—she had to run before she was blamed.

Before someone came after her, she must try to escape. Frantically she dressed for the out-of-doors, adding an extra layer of dress rather than carrying anything. She gathered up a little money and a comb.

She must keep herself presentable. She had to eat to keep up her strength. Somehow she would find Semyon, if she had to infiltrate London's most dangerous hells to do it. Damnation—she would parade through them naked if she had to.

Victor had to be a habitué of such places, given the business he was in. Her stepbrother's wickedness knew no bounds.

She was sure her lover had been kidnapped and taken away to get to her in the end. He would be used as bait to catch her—at least it meant he would be kept alive until she walked into the trap, wherever it was. Certainly not in a parlor of some quiet house. And not in a prison that was run by the authorities, packed with rabble.

If she could find Victor, she could find Semyon. She prayed that his animal instincts would draw her to him somehow.

With the Pack in a huddle around the table in the great hall and far from merry, she stole down the stairs and out the front door.

No one saw her go.

She kept to the side streets, avoiding the neighborhood of Mayfair, where the little house was, her head down and a cloak drawn over her conspicuous hair.

Her steps moved swiftly over the cobblestones and her mind raced ahead, trying to think of where to go first. She stopped by a small public garden, not cheered by the bleak prospect of bare trees and half-frozen earth. But it was secluded and she could gather her thoughts.

Angelica sank onto a bench. She thought and thought, and something did come to mind, although the memory made her recoil inwardly.

Mr. Congreve had subscribed to a kalendar put out by the brothel keepers. It listed specialties and the women who offered them, and even fees. Such a guide would be a start. She could make inquiries.

The madams would assume she was looking for such work.

She could endure their appraising stares if it meant finding Semyon.

Angelica dashed away tears, knowing that his heart would break with grief if he should see her reduced to that. But what could he do to save himself or her?

He would be shackled somewhere as surely as she had been, his wolf powers dwindled to nothing.

She thought more deeply, trying in effect to enter her stepbrother's mind and imagine what he would do. His taste ran to whipping and watching—she knew that only too well.

That narrowed the question of where Semyon might be. But she would have to procure a kalendar like Mr. Congreve's and go to the brothels listed under that category. She steeled herself and walked in the direction of Soho, looking for a bookstore that catered to a disreputable clientele.

There were many, as it turned out. Her feet were sore and her hair bedraggled when she came to one that seemed safe enough for a woman to enter alone.

The proprietor glanced at her as she came in. "May I help you?"

The words for what she wanted froze in her throat. How could she say them aloud?

I am looking for a brothel kalendar. The sort that lists all the specialties. With addresses, if you please.

Angelica turned and fled, hearing the shop bell jingle in her wake. Two men coming in pressed against her and laughed coarsely when she shoved them away.

On she walked, her feet stumbling and rolling on the cobblestones. She tripped and caught herself against a wall. Behind it she heard a hideous groaning that terrified her until she realized it was a streetwalker with a man, who reached climax with a shouted curse.

She fought the urge to vomit. Then her hand touched a thick roll of wet pages stuffed into the wall and she pulled it away, not wanting to know in the least how it had come there or what it had been used for—ah! A sheet of it clung to her fingers and she shook them violently.

It drifted down and attached itself to her dress. Angelica saw what it was a moment before she dashed it away—a cover of a kalendar of the type she had sought to buy.

Filled with revulsion, she yanked out the rest of the pages from the wall and kept them rolled under her cloak as she hurried a little distance away.

The streetwalker came out from behind the wall and looked at her curiously, then went back to trolling for customers, lifting her skirts a little for the men passing by to show her dirty shoes and stockings.

Her raw voice echoed in Angelica's ears as she offered herself for sale. *Hexcuse me, sir. Looking for comp'n'y? Need a girl?*

Angelica felt pity that the streetwalker would have laughed at just as coarsely as the men who'd laughed at her.

She came to a tearoom and looked through the moisture clinging to the inside of the wide window—there were booths, she saw, and she had more than enough money for a cup of tea and a bun, and a room to let for the night.

The plump woman in the sleeved apron who ran the place showed her to a booth in the back and took her order, seeming pleased to have a soft-spoken customer who was obviously a bit of a lady. She left Angelica alone after she set down a large mug and a saucer holding the bun.

She had no clear idea of how far she'd walked or for how long, but her complete exhaustion hit her when she took a tiny sip of tea. Angelica cradled the mug in her hands, utterly grateful for its strength and bitter fragrance. Lucky enough at finding work as a maid, she'd put the thought that she would be upon the streets again far from her mind since her first bewildering days in the great metropolis three years ago.

How swiftly those years had gone by, she thought distractedly. Knowing then that she was free of her past kept her from thinking too much of her future. Or her stepbrother.

She took a bigger, mouth-filling, fortifying sip of the tea and let it warm her body and soul.

Like Semyon. Oh dear God.

She scrubbed at the tears that welled in her eyes with her hand, then remembered how dirty it was and what it had touched.

There was no end to misery once it began.

She slipped her hand into a pocket in the lining, hoping to find a handkerchief and finding banknotes instead and a solitary gold sovereign. How had the money come there? She had a feeling that Semyon had provided it in case she ran away, leaving nothing that would clink. There was no other explanation.

She hoped she looked respectable enough by the morrow to trade the notes for coin at the bank that had issued them. In the meantime, the sovereign would keep her.

Angelica looked around the tearoom. The other customers paid no attention to her and there weren't very many of them.

Gingerly, she took out the rolled pages she'd found in the wall and unfurled them in her lap.

Something for everyone, she thought dully, forcing herself to look over the salacious advertisements, blurry from the rain the paper had absorbed. She did notice that many of the brothels were clustered in the same area, and some types seemed to have taken over entire streets.

Those devoted to the various pleasures provided by whips, crops, and birch switches were not far from here.

All Are Welcome.

She could just imagine. Angelica steeled herself for the search as she finished her meager meal.

Head up, she walked through Soho, looking now for a room. Her previous experience and the wariness bred into her helped her find lodging for the night in a decent-seeming place.

Soho was not a neighborhood where people asked too many questions.

Angelica went up a crooked staircase behind the swaying rump of the landlady of the one she had chosen.

The candle in the older woman's hand revealed a clean but dreary room with sloping walls. There was a sagging bed and a few sticks of furniture. Angelica only nodded and went in, glad that no one seemed to notice she had only the clothes on her back.

A gold coin was a good thing to have. She blessed Semyon for putting it there and the notes, then fell on her knees and prayed for him when the landlady withdrew, leaving her with the flickering candle.

Then she cried as if her heart would break, thinking that it was she who had plunged him into such danger. His kinsmen had seemed as terrified as she was from her hidden vantage point above them on the stairs.

She'd heard no plans for a search fanning out across London, nothing intelligent said about where he might have been taken to—of course, they would not know where to begin since he had said little enough to them about her and what had happened, hoping they would leave well enough alone.

It was all her fault. She vowed a dire vengeance upon her stepbrother and the man known as St. Sin.

Tomorrow she would begin her search. She knew no one from the house in St. James's Square would come looking for her. She was, as ever, on her own.

"Have you seen him?" She described Semyon yet again, at the ninth brothel of the evening, not saying his name.

The madame shook her head. "Naow. You might try next door." She looked Angelica up and down. "Is he your husband then? We gets them and the single ones. All the same to me."

"I am not married."

"Lovely, you are. We do have an opening. New girl just died."

Appalled by the woman's casual tone, Angelica gave a barely noticeable shake of her head.

"Nothing catching, if that's wot you fear," the madame said. "A customer proved too strong for 'er."

Angelica hurried away. The next brothel and the one after that had no information to offer.

A cruel-looking man with a crop in his hand tapped it against his thigh and asked her to come in when he heard her out. She heard screams from inside.

She hastened from that evil place in tears.

How, she wondered, had Semyon ever found her?

Instinct. That was all the answer he had given her.

She had no idea if she possessed even a fraction of that quality, but then, she told herself, she was entirely human.

Still she remembered how his strength had seemed to flow from his hand into her every time he touched her.

If only his animal ability could too.

On she went, looking at the pages she had torn from the filthy kalendar. She vowed to stop in at ten more places by the end of the day and then go back to her room.

It had seemed difficult at first to believe that depravity was everywhere. More heartbreaking than that was the occasional glimpse she caught of young women she knew slightly, ones who had worked with her as maids or girls who clerked in shops.

These establishments devoured the unlucky and the naïve and, she had to admit, the naturally vicious.

They at least seemed to enjoy their work.

As the sun was setting behind a jumbled row of rooftops and chimneypots, she turned her weary steps to the lodging house.

A hack cab with a slouched driver half-asleep on the box rattled past her. She lifted her head and for the merest fraction of a second saw Victor in it.

He recognized her and . . . tipped his hat.

Angelica gave a cry as the cab went around a corner, tilting, then righting itself. She ran after it, heedless of her painful feet.

But it was soon gone, tilting around the next corner and vanishing utterly.

She trudged to the lodging house, filled with fear and hope. It seemed impossible that a face she so loathed was one she wanted to see, but it was true.

Up the crooked stairs she went, throwing herself upon the bed and willing herself to believe that her search was not fruitless.

Semyon had to be in London. Somehow she just knew it. The question was where.

The next morning she managed to scrub herself clean and arrange her hair passably well. Or so it seemed in the cracked shard of a looking glass. She smoothed her clothes and cloak, and headed for the bank.

It was time to visit the more expensive establishments devoted to Victor's favorite vice. She had noted the ones who advertised to a female clientele. *Milady's Pleasure Is Assured. Discreet Afternoons. Ask For Best Rate.*

She would need better clothes and a visit to a hairdresser before any would let her through the door. And she would need to pay full price.

The teller was a grim little man who peered at the note and then at her, back and forth, several times in all, before he agreed to exchange the note for coin of the realm. Angelica strove to address him in dulcet tones, as if money mattered not a whit to her.

The sovereigns jingling in a bag tied to her waist were comforting, a reminder of Semyon's care for her.

Some were soon exchanged for new clothes and shoes, and she treated herself to a proper bath in a new place just for women. She was scrubbed and plucked and prettied up.

Angelica walked slowly to the first place on the new list and read the very small sign outside the building. *Miss Forsyth's Academy. Complete Instruction For Women.* She would not and could not give up. A clue that would lead her to Semyon might be found at this so-called Academy or someplace like it, and she had to persevere.

With a heavy heart, she lifted her hand to the bell and rang it.

A woman no longer young but still beautiful answered it, dressed in a high-necked gown. She had the ramrod posture of a schoolmistress but a marked sensuality showed in her face.

She looked intently at Angelica, until she quailed a bit.

"Yes?" the woman said.

"I have come for—for the instruction you offer," she stammered.

"Who recommended you?"

No pleasantries. No minced words.

Should she venture to say Victor's name? It might scare him off if by some chance he was here. On impulse, she said only, "St. Sin."

That softened the woman's mien to something like friendliness.

"Come in, then."

Angelica had the curious feeling that the woman was too near her without actually touching her. She sensed a heat along her back and behind, radiating with the same intensity of her gaze.

She hastened her steps and stopped before the only door at the end of the corridor. It swung open at an unseen touch.

Angelica entered and looked around.

The clients of the Academy were a well-dressed lot and most wore veils that made their features indistinct. They seemed to be of different ages. All held themselves tensely. She wondered at the strength of the needs that compelled them to seek out this place, and told herself that it was not her place to judge them.

The woman who had opened the door guided Angelica to a seat by herself, although she noted that the others did not talk at all.

Another woman came out from a different door within the waiting. She was more beautiful than the first and more stern, and there was a man by her side. He was tall and strapping but Angelica could not see his features under the half-mask he wore. He said nothing, only pointed to a client, seemingly at random.

She rose, trembling, and went to them, disappearing behind the closed door. The others stared straight ahead.

In time, Angelica heard sounds she knew. Very faint. But familiar. She hung her head, feeling her own buried shame and anger come to life again. She had no idea if she could bear to stay long enough to see what went on in this place.

Certainly she would not subject herself to their practices.

With all her senses heightened by fear and nerves, especially her hearing, she stopped breathing when a male voice came to her as if from several rooms away.

It was barely audible but it was unmistakably Victor's. The words were not clear, but that didn't matter. He was *here*.

She had succeeded in the first part of her quest.

Angelica rose from her chair and departed, mumbling a vague excuse to the woman who had greeted her.

The next few days she watched the place, walking by it in different garb but not going in. On the afternoon of the last day she saw Victor going in.

Angelica found a place where no one would see her and waited for him to come out. It took more than an hour, but she was ready.

He had a smile that she remembered only too well on his face. A vicious, superior smile. He was humming something under his breath when she waylaid him.

With a brick.

The thick-necked man she'd paid to wait with her put Victor into his cart and took him back to where he lived by the riverbank. There he tied him securely to a bed with no mattress and left Angelica to it. It was another hour before Victor came to.

"Guh—guh way," he said thickly. His eyes were bloodshot and there was a huge goose egg on his forehead.

"Where is Semyon?"

Her captive groaned in reply.

"Answer me, Victor. For the first time in my life, I have you where I want you."

"S-sorry. Dih . . . mean . . . hurt. S-sorry."

She waved a hand, staying a goodly distance away from him even though he was tied.

"Tell me where Semyon is."

"Nex' door."

"To Mrs. Forsyth?"

"For . . . yes."

She pondered her captive. It seemed unwise to leave him here, even though the thick-necked man had promised to sit with him. What if he was lying?

It had grown dark and he would have to go in the cart with her and the man. If Semyon was not at the Academy, then it would go hard with Victor.

Vengeance was vengeance.

Chapter 14

The three of them passed a long night in the ramshackle house by the Thames. By morning all the fight had gone out of Victor. Eventually he told her how the second abduction had been planned and carried out, and exactly where Semyon was—in a cellar at the house of St. Sin.

To stand guard, she would rely on Old Harry, the name du jour of her thick-necked friend, who wasn't old at all. He had called himself something else yesterday, which she had politely forgotten at his request, since he was her landlady's brother. Damn it all, she had to trust someone and so far he had proved himself worthy of it.

And he was strong, if ungentle. But both would come in handy to deal with Victor while she went out on necessary errands.

Justice of a sort had been done, but the hardest part was still ahead. Angelica had no idea if Sin would want his partner in crime back and somehow she doubted it. But if Victor could play a part in a devil's bargain, then he was still useful to her.

St. Sin, it seemed, was a madman. But even a madman had his rational moments and nothing would keep her from Semyon's side.

The thing to have was reinforcements. Old Harry knew the right blokes, he'd said, if the money was right. She went again to the bank and cashed another note, then returned to the house by the river, taking a circuitous route. It did not seem to her that she was followed.

Her captive needed food and drink as much as she did. She bought bread and cheese and ale and let it go at that. Prison fare was far worse and he ought to be grateful for his rough lodgings.

Angelica saw a tea stall ahead and stopped to buy some, choosing the cleanest of the available cups for her drink. She did not have time to be dainty and Harry's quarters were not set up for such niceties.

It occurred to her that the ramshackle house might not be his at all, but there was no help for that. They would be away soon enough, never to return.

She brought the food to Victor and served it to him in chunks on a piece of wood after his guard allowed him to have a hand free. He ate hungrily, stuffing his face and drinking down the bottle of ale.

Then he touched the goose egg on his forehead. It was turning purple but the swelling had gone down.

"Ow," he complained.

"Shut yer trap," Harry said. "That there is nuffink. I will give ye worse if ye can't be quiet."

Angelica watched Victor turn red in silence. At least her stepbrother knew when not to argue.

In another hour, the three of them were rattling in the cart to Sin's house. She'd had Harry put down thick straw for Victor, not to cushion his worthless bones, for which she cared nothing, but to ensure that he would not cry out with each jolt.

Old Harry had been very nice about letting him breathe, after all. The gag around Victor's head was tied with practiced skill, as were his hands. Angelica could not have done that or aught else of taking a man by force. As if Victor weighed nothing, Harry bagged him in burlap, threw him over his shoulder, and fastened the bag at four points in the cart.

"He's settled, missus," he said, giving a tug on one of the ropes. Victor groaned through the gag. "Shut up, you."

"Good. Then let's be off. Have you—"

"Aye. Me mates will come along by a different way, not that Annie here goes fast." He moved around to his mare, and stroked her coarse mane. "But we all likes a good brawl." He gave her a smile that was missing several teeth, then lifted her up onto the crude plank that served to carry the driver and the passenger of his cart.

He called a low gee-up to the horse and they drove away from the river.

"This one, is it?"

Angelica looked up at the house. All the curtains were drawn. She pulled the hood of her cloak closely around her face.

"Yes, I think so," she said quietly.

They stood out here, mostly because of the cart. There were no others about, and no street sellers. It was not a particularly fine neighborhood nor was it a rough one—the word for it was solid, and that described the houses as well.

He clambered down and assisted her off the plank.

Angelica exchanged a look with him as she stood upon the pavement. His bulldog courage showed in his stance—no one would harm her while he was there to stop it, not for any money.

Harry grinned at her, then looked down the street. Coming down the far end was a small gang of men like him, dock wallopers and the like, led by a huge fellow who raised his hand in silent greeting.

"In you go, then, missus. I shall stand right here."

She nodded, then mounted the steps. Taking the door knocker in her hand—it was as solid and plain as the house—she pounded it firmly and listened for footsteps within.

In another minute she heard them. The latch was pressed down on the other side of the door and it swung open.

There stood a tall man with a glittering gaze that moved rapidly over her face. He was unshaven and wearing disheveled clothes that looked like he'd slept in them. She caught a strong smell of whiskey and bile.

He looked at her curiously.

Angelica's breath stopped in her throat. She had not recognized him at first as her kindly confessor from the deconsecrated church. Yet St. Sin was the same man.

She stepped back in shock and almost tumbled, but he took her arm.

Harry moved forward threateningly. The tallest of his friends was now with him, she saw out of the corner of her eye.

"Let me go," she said desperately.

Sin did. "I thought you might stop by," he said after a moment, his tone weirdly congenial. "How nice to see you, Miss Harrow. Your stepbrother has told me so much about you, more than you told me yourself—"

"Don't," she said through clenched teeth. "That is him in the cart."

Sin craned his neck to look at the bag. "Is it? Aren't you a wonder, Miss Harrow. But then it looks like you had help."

He nodded at Harry and the tall man with him, then cast a glance at the rest of the gang, who had slipped into an alley.

"Semyon Taruskin is here in your house," she said. "Bring him to me."

Sin's laugh made him cough, and then he couldn't stop coughing for a few moments. He spat over the railing when his body stopped shaking, disgusting her.

He wiped his mouth, fixing his disturbing gaze upon her face.

"I do admire an intrepid woman," he said. "So is this to be an exchange of prisoners?"

"Yes." She didn't know whether to sic Harry and company on him, or stand her ground.

"But I have two to your one."

She gave him a confused look.

"There is Semyon and Antosha, the little fellow with spectacles. Smashed, I'm afraid. You might find that he has trouble seeing you." He paused. "Would you like to come in?"

Her mind was reeling, both from the present danger of her position and from finding out that she had told this evil man virtually everything about herself, seeking absolution from a stranger she thought she would never see again.

She would regret it for the rest of her life. Which would be short if she entered his lair.

"No," was all she said. "Send them out."

Sin took a step toward her, but stumbled and had to brace himself on the door frame. "Then I will come and say good morning to Mr. Broadnax."

As he went down the stairs, not seeming to mind if the neighbors saw his dishevelment, Angelica gave a silent sign to Harry and his friend to step aside.

The two men did but there was more than a hint of menace in the way they stood, watching him through squinted eyes.

Sin hummed tunelessly as he walked around the cart to the back. She stayed where she was but she could hear Victor's faint groan as Sin's hand went to the bag, looking for signs of life.

"One hundred pounds of potatoes does seem like a lot," Sin called to her, "but your price is fair. Done. How many shillings did you say?" He came back up the stairs.

"Bring me Semyon and Antosha," she whispered urgently.

"Not yet. And not here." He smiled broadly at her and spoke in a softer voice. "That is a good strong bag Victor is in but I see that he has wet himself. It was kind of you to provide him with so much straw."

Angela drew in her breath sharply. At least Sin wanted to bargain and he wanted his business partner back. Given his murderous nature, he probably wanted to dispatch Victor himself, but that was none of her affair.

"Where then?" she muttered.

Sin named an inn they had passed on the slow way here. "Do you know it, Miss Harrow?"

She nodded. "I saw it."

"It boasts a large courtyard where the stagecoaches stop. What with ostlers and grooms and drivers milling about, our meeting will hardly be noticed. Noon, then." He nodded at a church steeple that rose in the next block. "The bells are loud. You will hear them. Are we agreed?"

"Yes," she said numbly.

A minute after the hour, Harry drove them through the gates, his face grim. "I don't like this, missus. I'll be watching you closelike."

He pulled up and handed the reins to an ostler, then tossed a silver coin to the man when he'd jumped down, seeing to his mare himself. He rested a heavy hand on Victor and nodded to her. She could see the bag move. Good enough. They were ready. But where was Sin? He arrived late, and not in a cart. The carriage he drove himself was a closed one, and she could not see past the drawn curtains in the windows. He pulled up next to Harry's cart in a spot that—Angelica suddenly realized had been kept clear for him. The watching eyes of the inn's ostlers and grooms fixed on her, Harry, and Harry's tall friend. The other dockmen he'd enlisted drifted in unnoticed.

As Sin had said, the inn's courtyard was a busy place. Without her seeing exactly how, carriages and carts formed a wall of sorts that effectively hid their cart and themselves from everyone's view save that of Sin.

The tall man jumped down. He had put on a coat over his dirty linen and breeches, and boots, but he had not shaved and looked much the same.

"You are punctual," he said to her. The odor of whiskey on his breath was even stronger now. It mingled with that of hay and manure and the kitchen midden piled high with scraps that a stray pig rooted in, grunting.

Harry's narrowed gaze stayed on Sin, and his hand stayed on the burlap bag.

Sin smirked at him and went to open the door of the carriage. In it she saw . . . Semyon. And a slight man in spectacles that had one glass smashed and the other cracked. She gasped.

They were not tied or gagged but they were absolutely silent. Semyon's dark eyes stared at her fiercely. She thought irrationally that he too had not shaved, until she realized she was looking at the marks of the wolf.

His fur was growing. The puffy look about his mouth were from his fangs, growing too. She could see the white tips when his lips parted slightly.

Antosha shook his head and she realized that he was warning her to be silent. She gave an infinitesimally small nod.

"There they are," Sin said in a low voice. "Safe and sound."

"Let them come out," Harry growled. "We wants to see if they can stand. Mayhap you tied them up in there."

"No, not at all." Sin moved as if to clap Harry on the back in a friendly way, then seemed to think better of it. "Would you like to help them out?"

Harry shook his head. "Just let them out."

Angelica was grateful for his presence of mind in this dangerous situation. Yet Semyon had been brought . . . and he was coming out of the carriage . . . followed by Antosha.

The two men seemed stiff and she saw blood and dirt on their clothes, but they were—she wanted to scream the word—*alive*.

"There." Coming from behind her, Sin's voice was smooth. "You can see they are unharmed for the most part. We all took a nick or two, of course."

Semyon lunged forward just as a knife pressed against the pulsing vein in her throat and Sin twisted her arm behind her back. The pain was agonizing but she did not dare cry out. She saw Harry felled by a single blow from an ostler with hands like slag iron. Behind the row of carriages and carts was the sound of a deadly, almost silent scuffle. Then she heard running feet and hoped some had survived to tell the tale.

"Stay where you are," Sin said contemptuously to Semyon. "And you too, little man, or I will cut her throat right now and drench you both in her blood."

Semyon stopped, his eyes brilliant yellow with rage, his chest heaving. It took several of Sin's henchmen to subdue, tie, and gag him, and then throw him back into the carriage. Antosha got the same.

And finally it was her turn. She was trussed with utmost

swiftness and gagged dangerously tight and then thrown on top of them.

The two men had been thoroughly beaten before they were returned to Sin's cellar. Chained in a niche at the other side of it, she saw them dragged by.

Hours passed or so she thought. The only light came from a tiny grated window that was sometimes dark and sometimes bright as she went in and out of consciousness. At some point her gag was removed.

She found she could not scream and supposed, hazily, that she had been drugged again.

That same night . . .

"Well. They are safely chained in the cellar for now," Sin said to Victor, dusting his hands as he came up from that dark place, followed by Hinch and two of the men from the inn's yard.

He paid the latter off with a handful of chinking coins and showed them out.

"And what of Old Harry?" Victor asked dully when Sin came back.

"Dumped by the river, beaten to within an inch of his life, along with his friends. Hinch and the others would have killed them if not for the pair of constables who happened along."

"Will we have to leave this house?"

"Of course. He might remember it, even after that many blows to the head."

Victor dragged himself up from the table and headed for the stairs. "I suppose I must go with you."

The next day found them ensconced in another house, a shabbier one in a nondescript neighborhood. Their three drugged captives, bound and gagged to be on the safe side, had made up the bulk of what came with them.

"Whose house is this?" Victor asked, hardly caring. The hour was late.

"The woman who concocts my potions," Sin answered. He pushed a rack of vials to one side with a great clatter, breaking one and releasing its contents, before he set down his glass of whiskey. "She owed me a favor."

Victor coughed from the smell of the broken vial. "What was in that?"

"Who knows? It's the only one without a label." Sin picked up a shard of it, cut his finger, and cursed. Then he found a rag and tossed it at the spreading liquid before it dripped on the floor. "I shall need stronger formulations to control Semyon. He has the strength of an animal."

"Did you not say the Taruskins have strange blood?"

"Yes," Sin said, looking at Hinch. "But it can still be spilled." He took a chair by the back and dragged it over to where the vials had stood.

"I suppose I should look at these. Maybe one will do."

"The drubbing they got ought to be enough," Victor pointed out.

"Perhaps," Sin said absently. "I did spare your stepsister. No black eyes or significant bruises. She has such white skin."

"Yes."

Sin hummed as he studied the other vials, which did have labels. "Ah," he said with satisfaction. "This one should prove interesting." He held it in midair and waggled it at Victor. "It enlarges the male organ. I had something amusing in mind to do with Semyon for our next orgy and this will help. If he does not die of priapism."

"And what is that, pray tell?"

Sin winked and gave his business partner a foul smile.

* * *

Angelica struggled to a half-sitting position, her palms making contact with a cold, gritty floor. She blinked, trying to make sense of what she saw.

Casks of wine and sherry, stacked. A jumble of discarded furniture, covered with a film of ill-smelling mold. Earth-filled bins for vegetables, smelling nearly as bad.

She heard the faint clink of a chain and looked at her ankles for shackles, fearing that her feet had lost feeling and running her hands over her legs to them.

There was no iron cuff or chain. For some reason, she was free.

But oh . . . so very weak. She saw a bowl of curdled milk with a sopping rag half in it and half hanging out so it touched the dirty floor. The sour stink of it made Angelica gag. She put a hand over her mouth and felt a crustiness around it. She wiped her fingers on her skirt and touched one to her tongue, dabbing at the crust, sniffing what she wiped off.

Dried milk. Someone had fed her with that rag, pushing it into her mouth, most likely. Making her suck when she could not eat.

To keep her alive. For what reason?

Again she heard the faint clink of a chain. She strained her ears toward the sound. Was she the only prisoner in this place?

If Semyon was here, she dared not call or even whisper to him. Any noise would alert a guard.

She tried to stand but knew in a moment she was too weak to do it, let alone walk. So she crept.

Her skirts impeded her. At least they were too damp from her time in this cellar to rustle. The thought made her realize that she had been here for some time.

She paused from her going on all fours and rested, almost

panting. Then she went on, going around an old pillar of fitted stone and saw them.

Semyon was chained to the wall. Beside him lay Antosha, obviously injured.

Semyon's bold yellow eyes pierced the gloom of the cellar. He was a wolf complete. But the iron collar around his neck, meant for the man he'd been when it had been clamped on, cut cruelly into his skin. Around it his magnificent ruff was tinged with blood.

She realized with a start that he was speaking to her but not in human terms. He could only manage the direct but silent communication of the thinking animal he was.

I cannot move, Angelica. The chain is too short.

"Let me help you," she whispered.

Your hands cannot break iron. But bring me water. It has been some time since they did. A woman fed you.

Hot tears rolled down her face and she dashed them away. Crawling, she found a bucket and an open keg of water she prayed was pure. She tasted a drop. It would do.

Angela filled the bucket and brought it back to him, positioning it so he could lap. It was not easy but he did it.

A sickening realization came to her: he might have died where he was had she not woken.

Get another bucket.

"More water?"

No!

His eyes and the very slight tensing of his belly over his back paws told her what he needed to do.

She found, not a bucket, but a large china pitcher with a cracked lip and pressed it over his penis. His pent-up urine streamed out into it, gurgling in the swell of the pitcher. His eyes closed.

Ahhh. I was about to burst. If I had let go, I would have sat in the puddle until my fur was soaked and my skin raw. Thank you.

What else had he had to endure? She felt ashamed that it was all she could do for him as she withdrew the pitcher, cleaning his organ a bit with the edge of her skirt.

Then she looked about for a place to pour it out. She pushed the pitcher carefully in front of her to the largest of the wine casks and pulled herself up by the spigot.

Someone had been sampling from the bunghole atop and put the cork back loose. She pulled it out and lifted the pitcher, then poured in the warm urine.

If Sin should drink to their deaths, she hoped he would choke on the first glass.

Angelica slid back down the floor and returned to Semyon. There was a trace, just a trace of laughter, in his stoic eyes.

"Are you hurt elsewhere?" she whispered. "Besides where the collar is?"

Only where I was beaten with a heavier chain than this. But I think Antosha has a broken arm. He fainted from the pain.

She crept to the curled figure of the smaller man, carefully removing his smashed spectacles, lest his eyes be cut by them.

"What can I do?"

Nothing at the moment. I think Sin is dead drunk upstairs. I heard him carousing hours ago.

"I will kill him!" she breathed and tried again to stand. She collapsed.

You are not strong enough.

"Then I must find a way to free you." She drew in sobbing breaths, feeling poisoned by the musty, fetid air of the cellar.

Free yourself first. Escape.

She would not. She was entirely to blame for everything that happened. She looked at Semyon, sitting back on powerful haunches, his ruff bristling with proud ferocity. He was absolutely motionless.

Angelica reached up a hand and slipped it between the collar and his skin. Where it was not cut, she massaged, easing the agonizing soreness as best she could.

For a few moments he let her and then she saw his eyes close. Tears rolled out and down his muzzle.

Never mind me, he said. *See to Antosha. Do anything you can.*

With utmost stealth, listening for the least sound from upstairs, she crept to him, wincing when she saw the odd angle of his arm. It was as if he was sleeping.

"Semyon, if I touch him, he might scream," she whispered.

There is something you can put on his tongue. Our captor does not work alone. The woman whose house this is mixes the drugs and he forces them down our throats. She is careless.

His eyes glanced to the side and stayed on a point. She looked that way and saw a corked vial left on a high ledge.

Use it. Try to sit him up so he breathes better. If he remains unconscious, you can set his arm.

"I have never—"

I will tell you how, Angelica. The cruel collar and chain rendered him as immobile as a statue. But his mind was as quick as ever.

Fighting her feebleness, she obeyed him and doctored Antosha as Semyon instructed.

"His injury might not be that bad," she said when she was done. The secretary was still unconscious but he had a better color and his breathing was not so ragged.

Good. Semyon stared straight ahead.

"Semyon—why did he not become a wolf like you?"

Semyon thought for a while, glancing at her only once. Then he closed his eyes again, resting from the effort of his stillness.

It seems to happen when I must protect you, Angelica. Sometimes from others. Sometimes from yourself. His chops curled in a sad smile for a fraction of a second.

"Oh, Semyon—what have I done?"

Nothing. You meant no harm and did no harm. A wolf naturally guards those he loves.

"I see," she murmured brokenly and cried again.

Do not weep. You must be as our women are. Strong.

"For you, I can be that," she whispered, stroking the fur on his face until he too wept again.

Chapter 15

They began to get an inkling of why their lives had been spared.

Overhead they had heard, for two days, running footsteps of tradesmen delivering all manner of things. Angelica, who was closest to the stairs, could hear the best and she crept to the others when night had fallen and St. Sin was once again dead drunk somewhere in the house above.

"There is to be a gathering," she said. "A louche affair, by the sound of it."

St. Sin is famous for the orgies he gives.

If they were to be forced to take part, the men would have to be unchained, she thought, and she, purged of the drugs she only pretended to take, holding the liquid in her mouth and spitting out most of it. Still, the little that she could not avoid made her mind behave oddly.

She had contrived in the hours between then and now to spread the links in Semyon's chain so that he could at least lie down, by patiently warming the metal in the warmest place she knew: between her thighs.

That trace of laughter had come into his golden eyes again when she stood by him to do it, his shaggy head against her hips.

But as he had said, she could not break the links.

Antosha had recovered enough to sit and breathe well, and when their captors checked on them, which was not often, feigned a much greater injury.

They expect him to die, was all Semyon had to say about it.

"None of us will die," she said in a fierce whisper when she had eased the chokehold that held him and sat down beside the two.

Then she heard loud voices arguing at the top of the stairs and made haste to go back to her place, curling around a somewhat fresher bowl of milk and the rag in it, closing her eyes.

"Where is the bitch?" Sin stumbled down the stairs with the woman close behind him.

"I keep her in a corner, sir—over there—"

His clumsiness was made worse by his rage. Over what, Angelica could not tell. She hoped he would not lash out at Semyon. It was easy to imagine his chops curling back over his fangs. One wrong move and Sin would lose a hand.

But Semyon would still be chained.

Sin contented himself with a kick at Antosha, it seemed. She heard the secretary cry out and closed her eyes more tightly, praying that he'd sounded agonized just to satisfy Sin's cruelty and not because he'd been badly hurt.

"Have you been feeding her?" he snarled at the woman following him.

"Yes, I give her that sop twice a day and she nurses the milk from it like a baby," the woman said, "but she grows thin. It is not enough, slight as she is. I don't think she is in her right mind anymore."

"Going mad? Good. Some might mistake that for passion," said Sin. His boots stopped at her head. She trembled and held her breath, hoping to God he would not kick her.

"She is worth a great deal, handled correctly," he said.

Angelica released an inaudible sigh. She remained limp as Sin's hands slid under her armpits and lifted her with no trouble at all.

"Yes, sir. Shall I wash her then?"

He walked back to the stairs with Angelica over his shoulders. "Not in this filthy place, Lucy. Take her to my room."

Angelica's empty stomach contracted in a painfully hard knot. She wanted to beat at him with her fists, bite, kick—she hung there like a broken doll, not daring to raise her head and look at Semyon and Antosha one last time.

"Very well," Lucy said.

"No, don't," he said, going up the stairs now. "I forgot that my true love is asleep in my bed. That won't do, will it, for her to find a dirty beauty in my bathtub? Although I would enjoy watching the cat fight."

He was in the kitchen now. Angelica stayed limp, looking down at square flagstone tiles colored dull red.

"You said no marks on this one," Lucy reminded him.

Sin left her behind as he took the stairs two at a time. He went down a hall to a room off the second landing and tossed her on the bed.

She sensed his hateful hand over her face when her head lolled to one side but kept her eyes closed.

Then his rough thumb pried open a lid and stared into her pupil.

This close, she could see the pits and scars that marred his face from his years of hard living, and the wrinkled flesh that bagged under his bilious eye.

She wanted to blink but he prevented her. His stinking

breath burned her open eye. Then his other thumb pried the closed lids of her other eye apart.

Looking at him was like staring into an evil sun that would blind her if she didn't turn away. Angelica shook her head free of his mean grip and moaned.

If they thought she was not in her right mind, she would act that way.

Sin drew back and raised his hand as if to slap her, but Lucy stilled him with a hand to his wrist.

"There, there, sir," she soothed him, "she is a bitch and no mistake. I will wash her for you. But tie her, please. She may find strength to run if the water invigorates her."

He got up, scowling fiercely at Angelica lying on the bed. She let her eyes roll up, showing him the whites.

"A good idea, Lucy. Your softest scarves, then."

Angelica was passive as her clothes were stripped off her and her wrists bound by Lucy.

Sin watched, his breathing ragged as more of her was revealed. Much as she loathed his gaze upon her, she knew her beauty was the one thing that might save her and Semyon and Antosha.

"Docile as a lamb, she is now," Lucy said softly. "Come along." She tugged at the scarves around Angelica's wrists, leading her to a small alcove where a bath was ready.

Sin was ready too, with a long scarf braided from several others. This he attached to the handle of the filled tub with knots he made wet and then jerked with all his strength. They could not be picked apart or even cut, she thought.

Would he watch her bathe, she wondered desperately.

He dipped the braided scarf in the bathwater, then kneeled to whip it around her ankle and fashion an intricate knot through her toes.

"There. She will not kick that off."

"Thankee, sir. It is just a precaution. I am stronger than she is. But I know how you value her."

Lucy brought Angelica close enough to the tub to step into it and lifted her leg for her.

The surprising warmth of the water nearly made her faint.

Lucy brought her bound hands to a rack with a towel on it and rested them there. Obediently enough, Angelica stepped her other foot into the tub.

Lucy dipped a large cup in the water and sluiced her down again and again. Shoulders, back, breasts, bottom—the water trickled over all of her. It felt so good that Angelica wanted to cry. When the cup was raised and lowered several times over her head, she did, letting her tears mingle invisibly with the water that cleansed her.

"She is magnificent," Sin muttered.

Angelica turned her face away. For a moment she had forgotten he was still in the room. Lucy soaped her wet skin assiduously, leaving trails of bubbles that slid down into the bath. "Yes, sir, she is a pretty girl. Have you a costume for her?"

"It has not arrived."

She prayed that he would leave his dull-witted assistant to her task and was glad when the slam of a downstairs door got him out of the alcove to see who it was.

Lucy continued to scrub her, humming.

"Lift your leg and put your foot on the rim."

Angelica would not and said nothing

The woman's eyes hardened. "Do as I say. Or I will call for the master. He will spank your bum for you, if need be. And he knows how to hurt without leaving marks."

She was forced to obey. Lucy scrubbed her ungently between the legs, as if administering a punishment she knew Sin could not see.

But she could not keep it up forever, and in due time she

went back to sluicing cleaner water over Angelica from two enormous ewers placed nearby.

Lucy walked backward to the door to call for assistance. "None of your tricks. I do think the water has revived you."

It had. Angelica stared mutely at her.

"Do not look at me so," the woman said uneasily. "Margaret! Sukie! Come here!"

Heavy shoes clomped up the stairs and two broad-shouldered girls came in, clad in plain aprons, their hair scraped back into close-fitting caps.

"You are to help me with this one," Lucy said. "Take a knife and cut the big knot first. The one on the handle of the tub."

The other girl stood guard, eying Angelica without much interest. The first one clasped the braided scarf in her hand when she'd cut the knot and together they led Angelica to a mirror.

Following Lucy's instructions, they washed her hair in a basin, taking some pains with it. But they were no more gentle than Lucy had been at the end, and pulled.

She made no protest. One girl wrapped her dripping hair in a thin towel and knotted that high upon her forehead.

"Stand up," she commanded.

Still bound, she was led to the bed and vigorously scrubbed dry all over. The room was not warm and Angelica shivered. Playfully, one of the hard-faced maids pinched at her nipple.

"Stop that," Lucy scolded her. "No messing about."

"Yes'm," the girl said, but sulkily. She glared at Angelica instead of the woman in charge.

The unexpected pinch was pure pain.

Was it a hint of more to come? Angelica told herself to be strong. If she could contrive to eat or drink something more substantial than milk-sop, it would help.

"May I have something to eat?" she asked tentatively.

"I will ask the master," was all Lucy said. "I think I hear him coming."

But the footsteps she heard were not his. The preparations for the orgy were in full swing but it was long before the guests were to arrive from what Angelica could gather from the muttering of the maids.

Her hair was unbound and carefully dried, then brushed to gleaming softness.

"Lovely, this is," said the other girl, the one who had not pinched her. She fussed with the shining locks, laying them over Angelica's shoulders.

The other maid looked enviously at her. "She is still a whore," she sniffed.

"Shall we dress her now?" the one playing with her hair asked Lucy.

"Wait for the master," the older woman said. "That is him."

Sin's booted feet made a tremendous noise on the stairs. The excitement of the impending affair put a spring in his step. He came in to the room and looked immediately and only at Angelica.

"She wanted something to eat, sir."

He let his eyes run over her nakedness. "Stand up."

The maid who didn't like her stepped forward and gave a yank upon her bound wrists.

She had to stand.

As if she were a slave in a market, he ran his hands over her flesh, assessing it. His hands stopped where her belly was concave, rubbing her there. "I do believe she is hungry," he said. "You can give her something."

He twined her silky hair around his other hand until it hurt and she gave a faint, inadvertent cry. Then he used it to turn her around, fondling her bare bottom in a rude way, shaming her in front of the watching maids and Lucy.

"This part has stayed nice and round, I see," he said, laughing. "Did you scrub it well, Lucy?"

"Yes, sir, front and back," the older woman said placidly. "She resisted me a bit but I got in there with that rough washcloth. She is very clean."

"Good work." He let go of her hair and her flesh suddenly. Angelic trembled. She had only her long hair to cover her and it wasn't long enough. If she were to use her hands to cover herself, she knew he would prevent her—or the maids would.

"Thankee," Lucy said.

"She is cold. Wrap her up—in a robe, a shirt of flannel, I don't care. She will feel like something from the fishmonger's stall if you don't."

His words surprised her. But she knew even more strongly that he had not said them out of kindness. She was his property, nothing more.

To be put up for sale to the highest bidder.

"Locked the door, did you?" Sin was shoveling food into his mouth, talking to Lucy.

"Yes, and left one of the maids with her," Lucy replied. "Angelica has no clothes to speak of but I wouldn't put it past her to break a window and shinny down a drainpipe."

"Mmf. You think of everything." He cleaned his plate, pushing a torn piece of bread around it to get the grease up.

Victor looked at the ceiling, feeling disgusted. The goose egg on his head was barely visible but it still throbbed.

"So, Victor. Do you think you can stomach watching your stepsister auctioned off?"

The younger man rose from the table, looking visibly ill. "No, Sin. Spare me that?"

With the greasy lump of bread crammed in his cheek, Sin gave a spluttering laugh. "Certainly. You can take the cloaks and coats instead, if you like. Hinch was going to do it, but I don't think fine ladies would trust him. You, on the other hand, are very good at imitating your betters."

Victor looked everywhere but at Sin, casting a glance at the cellar. He knew Semyon and Antosha were slowly dying down there, but he refused to go look at them, no matter how often Sin said he should.

But he did wonder about them. He had half-expected the entire clan to burst through the door and rescue their kinsmen at pistol point. He sighed and rubbed at his eyes. Since the moment of his assault at Angelica's hands and his rude imprisonment in the burlap bag—he was grateful to Sin for rescuing him from that, if nothing else—he had hardly slept.

Sin would not tell him who had survived on either side of the fight in the courtyard and Victor feared that there had been one too many witnesses. Someone must have informed on them, even if there had not been a constable for miles around. The matter must have gone to a magistrate and a case could be brewing against them right now.

Why did Sin never think of such things? Pimping and pandering did not disturb the peace, but brawling and murder—had there been one?—were not offenses that were so easily overlooked.

He knew only too well that Sin's contacts at court and his connections in government had saved the older man from prosecution, but no one's luck held out forever. It was just too bad that he, Victor, had joined forces with a devilish drunk when the glory days were over.

Sin's every-increasing appetite for vice was burning through what was left of their capital. He sampled the whores before he sent them out or taught them new routines, and of course they insisted on being paid—and there went the money. Victor had nothing to show for his initial investment. He had hesitated—Sin had not been wrong about that—when it came to his stepsister. He had not dissuaded his volatile partner from involving the so-called Pack of St. James.

As for the deep, dark secrets that supposedly swirled around the clan and the Taruskins, he had been told nothing more. Most likely it was half-remembered nonsense from some thundering melodrama Sin had once done, theatrics, that was all. He looked at Sin, red in the face from the wine and beefsteak he was putting away and laughing with Lucy, with nothing but loathing.

A noise from the cellar came to his ears.

By now Semyon Taruskin and that puny man who'd been captured with him had to be hanging on by a thread. He felt a flash of something like compassion for Sin's ill-use of them. God knew he had given up on his notion of using Semyon to play a role in the upcoming sex charade. No woman of breeding would want to be touched by a half-starved, crazed prisoner if it came to that.

"Done with the bone, Sin?' he asked acidly. "Shall I toss it down the stairs? I don't think they've eaten today, have they?"

Sin belched and looked insulted. "What? Don't tell me you suddenly have a tender streak. What do you care?"

"Never mind."

Sin chucked Lucy under the chin. "Want to take him down there and show him what they turned into?"

"No, sir, You may do the honors."

Sin stretched, then pushed away from the table. He picked up the chewed bone from his beefsteak and used it to gesture at Victor. "Shouldn't think you'd want to get your slender fingers dirty, Vic." He rose and walked to the top of the cellar stairs, flinging the bone.

It bounced off a wall, then fell with a thud on the floor they could not see. Victor just shook his head, folding his arms over his chest as Lucy followed Sin out.

Then, very faintly, he heard a growl from the cellar.

One or both of them must have gone entirely mad. Death could not be far off.

Chapter 16

Angelica suppressed a shudder as she looked at the costume laid out for her. It consisted of little but straps attached to each other in unmentionable places. There were boots that matched it with heels almost too high to walk in and a hundred buttons upon the back of each. There was a mask that was almost elegant, also made with straps that would pull it tight to her face and emphasize her eyes.

The costume was utterly tawdry and looked something like a corset ripped to pieces. Not even her recent forays into the debauched underworld of Soho and her necessary inspection of the racy advertisements in the kalendar had shown her anything like it.

As to where she was to wear it and who would see her—that was an open question. She suspected the answer was ugly.

It didn't matter. Semyon was chained in a foul cellar, unable to assume human form and attempt an escape. At least he would not see her degraded.

Angelica vowed to think only on what might help her get them all to freedom.

She heard the preparations for the party downstairs become louder and more rushed. There would be a great deal of drinking.

No matter what, that alone greatly improved their odds.

She turned as Lucy came in and extended her hand. "Give me your robe. The master wants you ready before we begin."

Angelica sighed inwardly and let it slip from her shoulders onto the floor. She meant to pick it up but Lucy seemed to think that she'd let it puddle at her feet to personally humiliate her. She bent and whipped it up and away like a soft lash.

That could not be helped, Angelica thought darkly.

Lucy marched to the bed and picked up the strapped corset. She seemed intimately acquainted with it.

She held it out to her at the level of her hips. "Step in. And be quick about it."

Angelica had to obey. Anything else would cost her dearly. She put her hands on Lucy's shoulders and stepped into what seemed to be leg openings.

Lucy gave a curt nod, then pulled the thing up with a vicious jerk.

It hurt her in the tenderest place, but she would not give the maid the satisfaction of knowing that. Angelica stared at a point over Lucy's heavy shoulder, letting herself be mercilessly pushed and pulled and buttoned and strapped.

"There," Lucy said, stopping for breath. She gave Angelica a little push toward a tall cheval glass. "Look at yourself."

Angelica had to. Her naked breasts jutting out was the first thing she saw—a thick strap ran directly beneath them. From it descended two more straps that attached to a high girdle banding her hips. The V of this was what Lucy had pulled so hard, almost parting her labia.

"Turn around," Lucy barked.

When Angelica did, the other woman handed her a hand mirror.

"Look at yer arse. Not bad."

Angelica examined the rear view of the corset in the mirror. It lifted her buttocks into high, firm curves that were separated by a strap too. The back of her waist was crisscrossed with still more straps that pressed tightly into her yielding flesh.

Out of the corner of her eye she saw Lucy approach her with the final indignity: a collar of iron, identical, though smaller, to the one that been clamped around Semyon's neck.

"You will wear it and like it," Lucy said softly, noting the flash of fear in Angelica's eyes.

One of the younger maids came in to assist her. She had evidently been waiting outside should there be any trouble, and she seemed to Angelica somehow larger now and more ominous, though her plain apron and cap had not changed. It was her manner.

She wondered if these servants were to play a role in St. Sin's erotic show or if they merely watched. They were not in the least pretty but strong and almost brutish for women. To some debauchees, those qualities were just as attractive.

Angelica had learned much that was unsavory in the last several days.

The younger maid gathered up Angelica's hair and twisted it into a tight knot with her hands, controlling her with ease as Lucy clamped on the collar.

She essayed a breath. There was just enough room around her throat.

Lucy put a finger through the ring that was soldered to it. "This is for your chain. How do you like that?"

Any answer was likely to anger her. She said nothing.

The younger maid stood still while Lucy went to fetch a little dish of hairpins. These she jabbed in, scratching Angelica's scalp painfully more than once.

She reminded herself of the torture of Semyon, sitting still, in a chained collar of his own, and her own pain seemed like nothing.

Lucy stood back, her hands on her solid hips. "You can let go of her hair. But put your finger through that empty ring. Just in case she bolts."

The maid obeyed and now she was face to face with Angelica.

Again Lucy went in search of things for the hair and returned with long, wicked-looking sticks enameled in black. She added these decorations in a crisscross arrangement that echoed the back straps.

It seemed to please her.

"And now for them boots," she muttered. She kicked a footstool in Angelica's direction, picking it up when it rolled and setting it directly in front of her with a thump. "Step on that."

Angelica did as she asked.

"Not high enough," Lucy said. "Sukie, you get on all fours in front of her—don't look at me like that."

The maid hitched up her skirts and did what Lucy said.

"Now you stretch out your leg over her back so I can put one on. They are snug fitting."

At that moment St. Sin returned in a suit of impeccable evening clothes. There was an unholy fire in his eyes when he came upon the three women.

"Lucy, what are you doing?" he asked.

"Getting this one dressed."

Sin looked about for a chair and finding one, sat in it and leaned back. Angelica refused to meet his gaze.

Lucy kneeled and struggled to get the thin leather of the boot over Angelica's high-arched foot but in the end she managed it.

She took hold of the heel and the toe and pushed aside the leather that would be buttoned around her calf, setting Angelica's foot squarely upon the maid's broad back.

Sin grinned. "Very nice. We might make this part of the show."

Lucy paid him no mind as she began to hook the buttons closed with a small implement that jabbed Angelica too often to be accidental.

When the row of buttons was hooked up, her calf was completely covered in the leather.

"Now the other," Lucy sighed. "Stand on the done-up one."

Angelica set her foot in the high-heeled boot upon the carpet and wobbled dangerously. Lucy caught her under the arms and just stood there.

"Move," St. Sin said to Lucy. "I want to see her, not you."

"Yes, sir. Where is the other girl? I need her." Lucy called for her, still holding Angelica. Her closeness was unbearable but there was nothing for it. Angelica still would not look at Sin, knowing that his eyes were devouring her.

The other maid came in and held Angelica up while Lucy set her bare leg again on the back of the maid who stayed patiently where she was, though her face was sullen.

"Quite a tableaux," Sin said. "Beauty Attended by Three Beasts."

The maids did not seem to dare to answer back. He kept right on watching lazily as the second boot was put on and hooked up.

"Stand up," Lucy said.

Angelica took her foot off the maid's back, feeling sorry for her. She felt dangerously unsteady and much too tall. She was nearly as tall as Sin, who got up and came to stand in front of her. He seemed to take a perverse pleasure in not actually touching her.

But his constant, sweeping surveys of her bare flesh were just as bad.

She teetered on the high, high heels.

"Walk," he said. "Practice. You don't want to fall down when you are on the auction block, do you?"

She mutely shook her head.

"Then walk to the cheval glass, turn, and come back."

Angelica managed it, but how, she did not know.

"Very good," he said, a note of surprise in his voice. "Try it again."

When she had taken her first step, he seemed to change his mind. "Strut instead. Can you do that? Make it seem as if you like a hundred pairs of eyes on you. Make this"—he pinched the high curve of one buttock, making her flush scarlet with embarrassment—"jiggle a little. Sway and strut. The heels should strike smartly with every step. You will be on wood, and not carpet."

"All men tonight, is it?" Lucy asked.

"Mostly. Some women."

"Wives?"

"A few. Shut up, Lucy. I am instructing Angelica, as you can see."

The maid stepped back into the darker part of the room and she brought the younger women with her.

It was as if she were entirely alone with Sin. Angelica had not imagined that she would miss the company of the three others but when she could not see them, she did.

From inside his coat pocket, Sin produced a riding crop. He touched it to his lips and then waved it over her bare breasts. All she could feel was a tiny slice of moving air. Again, he had not touched her.

She realized that it was the expectant flinch he enjoyed most. She had to do her utmost to control it.

"Walk again," he said, "back and forth. To me and away from me."

She obeyed.

"Yes. Like an automaton," he said. "But you have a natural grace that makes your walk irresistibly sensual. One more time, Angelica. Then stand in front of me."

She did as he requested, her mind elsewhere the entire time. When she stood in front of him, her legs were together. The crop tapped the carpet between her toes. Inch by inch it moved up.

She did not want him to touch her with it, would not let him. She stepped her feet apart slightly.

The rising crop reached her knees.

"How demure you are," he said. The tip of the crop lifted and her knees moved apart too.

Up it went. Her booted legs made a strong inverted V. Inside this the crop whistled as if he were drawing her in the air, imagining her somehow.

Forcing her to do his obscene bidding in front of three silent witnesses.

"Turn around," he said in a low voice.

She stood stock-still.

"If you will not, we will make you," he said in a pleasant voice.

Lucy started forth from the shadows and Angelica reluctantly turned around. The atmosphere of growing menace did not incline her to argue.

She stood there for no longer than a moment.

"Put your hands on your hips—there, that is not hard, is it? And the effect is very pretty."

If he could only see the hate in her eyes. The stance fit the emotion. That was some comfort.

"Now bend over." His voice was low.

Angelica hesitated, beginning to tremble again. She was feeling faint, had never been brought the food she'd timidly asked for, but again—the two in the cellar had it far worse than her.

"Ah, there is the jiggle," he said approvingly. She took a very deep breath and forced her trembling away.

"Where were we, Lucy?" he asked.

"You wanted her to bend over and she didn't."

Was Lucy hoping she would be punished in front of them all? The man in the chair had other ideas.

"Yes. Over you go." The tip of the crop tapped her hands off her hips one by one. She didn't like it when it hadn't touched her, she feared it now. "Clasp your knees," he directed her.

Angelica bent over, knowing how much of her he could see and felt scorching flames of humiliation lick at her face and neck.

Ever so slowly the searching crop traced over her bare buttocks, prodding between, into where Lucy had jerked the corset's nether strap.

"Do you like that?" he asked her in a rasping tone.

She blurted out an answer without thinking. "No."

"Good. Stay bent over. *I* like looking at you this way." She could hear the unpleasant smile in his voice. His crop continued to prod and tease. "Drop your head. Let it hang. You are very tense, my dear."

She gritted her teeth and did that too. The probing tip of the crop touched her lips.

"Open up, my dear," he said in a whisper. "Take it in your mouth. Suck the tip."

She was desperately afraid but knew she could not overpower him or run in the treacherous boots. He prodded and she parted her lips, taking just the narrow tip of leather into her mouth.

"Suck," he said again. "Small tugs that I can feel in my hand. Make a little noise."

She wanted to scream, but she had to concentrate on holding the tip in her lips. She told herself it was only a thing. Not a man. Not flesh. She sucked it and murmured false enjoyment with every pull and tug.

"Mmm. Mmm. That's right. Very good. You learn quickly, Angelica."

He withdrew it and she straightened before he could tell her no, her spine aching. To ease it, she put her hands on the small of her back and rubbed it, whirling around but only at the waist when his hand rested warmly on her behind.

He took it off and gave her a final, approving tap with the crop, drinking in the blazing fury in her eyes. "You are quite the finest woman I have ever seen, Angelica."

"Go to hell." Her voice was murderously quiet.

"If I can bring you with me. Do you want to go?"

She shook her head in silent fury and moved away from him, quickly blocked by the maids. Sin gave her a gentlemanly bow and left the room.

Chapter 17

With Lucy holding her elbow, Angelica made her way down the stairs, once again robed. She fought her fear of what awaited her beneath every step of the way.

She sent a prayer heavenward for Semyon and Antosha. Still she believed that they could escape a drunken riot, as this was bound to become.

Serving men carrying punch bowls between them went down the hall at the bottom of the stairs. Cold food on trays followed that.

She noted an aspic in the shape of a naked woman arranged on a gigantic platter. The aspic jiggled obscenely. Of course.

Lucy steered her to a side door where she would wait.

And, she thought, make a dash for it if at all possible. But the stolid Lucy didn't leave her there.

She merely asked a footman for two chairs and pushed one at Angelica, then sat in the other.

"Master Sin said you was to watch and learn," Lucy said, as prim as a governess. "Your stepbrother will not be joining us. He is not well."

She was grateful for that.

The guests, and there were many, were engaged in very loud conversation. Their attire was not shocking, but revealing to an extreme for the women. Bodices seemed to hang from the nipples beneath. Slits up the side gaped and some of the men were already exploring the thighs beneath.

The men were not particularly attractive but they seemed well heeled. To a man their breeches were tight.

Angelica suspected some had resorted to padding. How the company would laugh to see a false cock revealed by some eager hussy. The thought was repellent.

It was almost a pity to acknowledge it but St. Sin was the best-looking man of them all, much as she loathed him.

Never mind, she told herself. It would help her to control her emotions and to be as objective as possible. Only then could she seize the right moment and escape.

She noted how the women seemed to grovel a little when Sin walked by. He stopped at every little table crowded with chairs and the knots of people talking away as well. Some women put out their hands for him to kiss and arched upward as if to give him the best possible view of their bosoms.

He examined all the female flesh on display with the same avid interest.

Some of the men went so far as to pull up the skirts of the women sitting with him, as if for Sin's appraisal. He stroked a powdered thigh here, kissed a pretty foot sans slipper raised high to his mouth—and looked down at the bare pussy beneath when he did.

She realized that he was making a selection among them.

The women he chose by his touch, three in all, went up upon a low stage. A hush fell over the noisy crowd.

It seemed some sort of play or contest was about to begin. Angelica could not tell which.

The first woman lifted her skirts slowly, revealing a neat

patch of fur to wild applause. She turned round, displaying her dimpled bottom, and then managed to hold up her skirts with her elbows and fondle her buttocks with her hands at the same time.

A neat trick and the crowd loved her wantonness.

Sin jumped on stage and led the applause as she ran off.

The second woman was blond and pale. She simply slipped her dress off her shoulders and stood there stark naked, glowing white. Angelica thought the effect was achieved through some clinging powder applied to her body, it seemed so unnatural. But the people watching again called out in admiration. Her cunny hair was so fine as to be invisible and the pink slit showed well under it. She, apparently, was just there to be looked at like a statue, but in time she too departed to applause.

The third woman reached out a hand to Sin and kneeled before him when he took it. A supplicant, Angelica thought. Like the women of the academy, craving instruction of the most sensual sort.

The crop came out from his coat, clasped in his hand, and he held it high. There were animal-like noises of approval, roars from the men and cries from the women.

With just the tip, he hooked the hem of her gown at the back and lifted it as she buried her face in his breeches. His other hand kept her head there, her features hidden, commanding her. As if he had much practice at the game, he drew the light gown up and up until he could catch the hem in his thumb and pull the gauzy material over her face like a veil.

The action revealed her nakedness. A much more profound hush fell over the onlookers. Her body was beautifully formed and a-tremble with eagerness. Angelica leaned forward, hearing and not quite hearing—yes, she was asking him humbly for a whipping.

And Sin began. He was indeed skilled at his trade. There

were no marks to be seen, but the woman's skin glowed delicately pink.

Each lick of the expertly wielded crop seemed to excite her. Her invisibility under the veil he had improvised for her seemed to heighten it.

In good time he stopped, permitting her to rest, naked before the silent crowd. He looked out and spoke to them.

"Who is her husband?"

A man rose and went up to the stage, running his hands over her and lifting her with Sin's help, still veiling her face. She was nearly limp with pleasure at being handled by two men but it was her husband who did the honors.

He unbuttoned his breeches and out sprang an organ that was remarkable for its length and thickness. This he positioned and plunged into her cunny, redoubling his strokes with vigor when she cried for all he could give.

The couples in the room moved closer to each other. The husband, crying out, climaxed with his young wife, her face still hidden, when he reached under her dress to bring her along, manipulating her most intimate flesh in his fingers.

Somewhere a light that was mounted high then turned to Sin.

He was, as before, impeccably dressed, and just stood there, his hands folded over the handle of the crop. Angelica looked at Lucy. The maid gazed with rapt attention at the stage, where the married couple in the shadows kissed and caressed and adjusted their clothes.

In the audience, the couples at the tables and the standing ones were doing the same, some joining in threes and even fours for sensual, uninhibited play.

Angelica uncrossed her legs. Her upper thighs were wet. The tight, corsetlike garment she had on had proved stimulating, even though she had only watched. It was not humanly possible to be as cool as she wished but she must try again.

"That was the free show," Sin said in a booming voice. "I will take bids later. We are starting high—I swear to you that she—and he—will be worth it. High bids, gentlemen. And ladies," he added, not quite as an afterthought.

The party continued, a dreamlike vision that was sometimes tender and sometimes obscene. It was impossible to remember the combinations of bodies and positions—it became a blur.

A wearying fog enveloped her until she heard Sin's voice. Too near. She struggled to sit up—and where had Lucy gone? She had no idea how much time had passed. Angelica tried to move and she realized she had been tied to her chair and could not.

"Get those two out of the cellar," she heard Sin say. "The earl wants to choose his own bottle of wine, the pretentious fool. I promised him a tour."

"That big one is lunging at his chain," Hinch replied. "The other one will be dead by dawn, mark my words."

"The drug has worn off then—and how did the chain get long enough for him to lunge?—oh, never mind!"

Hinch made some answer, but Sin talked over it. "Shut up. And tell Lucy to drench him in cold water when you get him out of there. There is a tub of it around here for the punches and ices. His blood is too hot."

"But if—"

"Do as I say!"

Angelica's eyes widened with terror. It was not long before she heard Semyon's deep, wolfish growl and saw him dragged past by three strong men.

He did not see her. Antosha must still be too weak for anyone to care about him, she thought, picking at the scarves knotted around her wrists and the chair. She could not undo them, not to save her life.

"Don't know why he don't just shoot the beast," she heard Hinch say. The other men joined in.

"Sin says he ain't an animal, Hinchy."

"Bloody hell! He bites!"

Semyon's growl reverberated underneath it all as Angelica sagged in her chair. As far as she could tell, Semyon's strength was too sapped to fight. He gave a howl that slowly ebbed away as he was manhandled, judging by the complaints and the sound of sloshing, into water.

Soon enough, the howl ebbed away. Had they cooled his blood to the freezing point and killed him?

Angelica pulled frantically at the knots that held her, knowing as she did that she could never fight so many men to save him. There were a hundred more in the main hall who would help Sin and not her.

The enclosed place where she was trapped was hot and stuffy, and her mind whirled unceasingly. She could not keep her chin up. Someone came in—Lucy?—and untied her bonds. Angelica tried to stand and fainted.

She woke on the same stage where the women had been. But despite her costume, she was not the only attraction.

Semyon had been returned to his human form. Whether the ice had done the trick or another potion forced down his throat, she had no idea. Probably both. He seemed slightly groggy when he looked her way—and she realized with shock that he didn't seem to recognize her.

His eyes, hazel again and not the piercing true gold of a wolf, only glanced at her with indifference, then away.

So his protectiveness toward her, the quality that had made him turn full wolf in the first place, was no longer there. Sin, who knew more than most about the clan, had broken through some weak place in Semyon's beleaguered mind.

And here they were on stage before a crowd of dissolute drunks.

Sin, leering, stood to one side. He motioned her to rise up and walk to Semyon. She noticed at the moment that the iron collar was still around his neck.

Her hand flew to her own neck. She wore the matching one. Slowly, mesmerized by Sin's evil eyes, she walked to him. He held up a length of chain for the watching people and linked her to her lover. They had room to move apart but they did not.

Semyon stood there, not looking at her now. And she would not look at him.

Sin gestured for applause, pointing first to Semyon. The bright, sharp little claps from the women seemed to sparkle through the air because Semyon was stark naked and utterly unashamed of it. It was his air of wildness that intrigued the watching women. Here was a man untamed, big and massively hung, with a feral look that made them scream like animals.

Sin took out his crop to point to Angelica and the men took over, slapping their thighs into the bargain as they clapped thunderously.

"Just walk," he told her, his eyes glittering.

She raised a hand to the collar and the chain that linked her to Semyon.

"Walk around him. He will have to follow."

She took a step, then another. He turned like an automaton. Their bodies on full display from every angle evoked screams and shrieks. She hated every second of it, hated the heedless, faceless crowd.

Every now and then Sin's crop touched her body. She stopped once and he laid it across her nipples, pressing the thin but flexible rod deeply into her breasts. That got the loudest applause yet.

He hissed at her to bend over. She ignored him. The next time she passed near to him he grabbed her, but Angelica had

had enough and bit his hand so hard she drew blood. Looking at the dumb misery in Semyon's face renewed her resolve to escape before this dreadful night was through.

Sin hissed with pain. Swiftly and with all his strength, he folded her over one arm and swung her in the air, her booted legs dangling.

He raised the crop. The crowd cheered him on. Down it came. Again and again. They counted the stripes she took and roared for more. Semyon stood looking on, his eyes glassy, weirdly subdued, as she twisted her body to see him. Angelica hung her head and endured the public punishment in silence. It clarified her mind to the highest degree.

She stepped neatly away when he let her down and bowed to her admirers. Angelica knew she would be up for sale soon. There was no man in the room but Semyon who compared to Sin in strength. The richest men here were probably the puffy-faced ones with a touch of gout.

One of them would ultimately buy her and free her. That was why they were here. And if she could put on a show to end all shows with Semyon, drugged though he was, her lover might go with her.

Two for the price of one. They would come back for the injured man in the cellar and remove him if it meant killing someone.

Angela moved closer to Semyon and began running her hands over his body. The muscles under his skin rippled at her touch as she caressed his arms, his chest, his taut groin.

With a firm hand that delighted the watching men, she made him turn around and caressed his buttocks, from the splendid muscle they were made of to the subtle hollows in the sides.

Then she bent to stroke his powerful thighs, knowing that the boots made her legs look impossibly long and slender compared to his oaken strength.

The best for last.

She had found her mark, an older man with diamond studs and eyes that popped. He watched more avidly than anyone else and he had come alone. No whining wife to tell him no. He reached into his waistcoat and pulled out a wad of banknotes, nodding at her.

Angelica smiled politely back and began to stroke Semyon's cock. Even when not erect, it was an impressive sight and her attentions to it were making it longer and thicker.

"Do you want us?" she cooed to the old fellow watching. "Both of us?"

"Yes, my gel. Yes, I do." He glanced at the master of ceremonies. "Name your price, man."

Sin looked at the wad of banknotes and shook his head. "Twice that for two," Sin said. His fierce glare told Angelica that he was furious at being upstaged by her. He seemed determined to get in the way of what she was doing.

How far could she go? The fact that she knew no one here emboldened her. There were worse fates, she thought wildly.

Sin moved forward, egging on the watchers. Their screams and caterwauling rose to a deafening pitch. The servants in attendance upon them plied them with more drink, moving through the room as if on the lines of an invisible, evil web with Sin at its heart.

She was trapped in it, might die in it. His method was both violent and patient, but it was based on madness, which played out now in isolation and sexual intimidation. After the failure of her attempt to rescue Semyon and the untold hours imprisoned in this house, she had no sense of the outside world. Her clothes had been stripped from her as if Sin had stripped her skin. The house in St. James's Square, the half-men, half-wolf Pack, the very morning when Semyon and Antosha had been taken seemed like a distant dream.

Some trick of the light made him appear suddenly much larger, even to her.

Angelica fought a feeling of despair. To escape, St. Sin would have to be overcome. She could never do it alone and the two men she'd thought might somehow aid her were broken and defeated.

She had an idea what could happen to performers at such a show, trotted out to be sold. If they were not, they would be damaged goods to be unloaded cheaply or killed. Sin was under suspicion of more than one murder. And Sin seemed maniacally intent on thwarting her sale. Semyon would be thrown back in the cellar to perish after tonight, along with Antosha, their bodies left upon a dung heap.

But . . . if she could reawaken the wolf nature within Semyon . . . there might yet be a chance. She searched his face, looking deep into his eyes as her hands resumed their caressing motion. As if there were no one watching at all, she felt a tremor begin deep within his body.

His hand caught her wrist. "Angelica," he whispered. "What are you doing?"

Good God. There was a flicker of his soul in his eyes, but it was barely there.

"Bringing you back, Semyon. Where are you? It is as if your eyes do not see this room—"

She heard the crop whistle through the air before a sharp sting hurt her shoulder. Sin was bellowing lewdly at the onlookers, asking them if she deserved it.

The older man who'd wanted her and Semyon shook his fist. "Do not hurt her, man! She is mine! I have paid for her!" He waved the notes frantically, standing up to shout at Sin.

"Not enough," Sin said contemptuously. "What else am I bid?"

Angelica looked out, not seeing much in the crowded, dark room. Then an oddly familiar voice shouted out, "A thousand pounds more! For me and my wife!"

"Then it is two thousand more! You get both!" Sin called.

She knew that voice from somewhere, but her mind would not put a face to it. Angelica peered out desperately. Whoever it was—the voice was male—might be their savior tonight.

"One thousand, five hundred!" the bidder called.

She wanted to scream at Sin to say yes and call it done. How much more he would ask for, she did not know. But there was a point past which the richest man would not go—not when pleasure could be found so cheap all over London.

A mad dash with their purchaser out to a waiting carriage, past Sin, his pockets stuffed with money. The client would expect a private show at home or in some hidden hell like this, but they would not get it. They were far from safe in a stranger's carriage or house, but the odds were slightly better that they might escape and live.

"I take it you are happily married," Sin called back to the unseen bidder, joking with him, trying to soften him up. "How many husbands and wives are here tonight?" he asked the laughing crowd. "Is matrimony as dull as all that?"

He got a chorus of rude answers and catcalls.

"Any other couples in the bidding?"

"One thousand, five hundred," the familiar voice said again.

"Bah. These two are worth more." He gave Angelica's calves a swift lash with the crop. "Much more!"

Still chained to Semyon, neck to neck, she stumbled, but caught herself on his unyielding body. She could not fathom what was going on in his mind.

Was he even capable of thought? It seemed to her that he flickered in and out, as if he were no more than a picture in a magic-lantern show and not a real man. Not a wolf, either.

"Her alone!" a different man cried.

"No. They will go together or not at all!"

The bidding became frenzied but the raises were too small to satisfy Sin's greed—or his madness.

Then the voice she knew called out from the darkness. "Two thousand!"

At last. She looked desperately at Sin. Would he take the bid he'd asked for?

He looked at her menacingly and at Semyon. "Stroke him again. Make him hard. Work for the money, Angelica!"

Bewildered, desperate, she put herself into it, stroking first, then clawing. Drawing thin lines of blood in his skin that made the crowd scream again.

She slapped him, hit at him, and suddenly saw the blankness in his eyes vanish. The soft mingling of brown and green turned to piercing yellow and his pupils changed into oval slits, pointed at either end like tiny daggers.

Sin's endless exhortations to the crowd grew wilder and more obscene as he pointed at their bodies in place after place, even lashing at both of them with his crop.

Semyon didn't flinch and that made Sin angry. He grabbed the chain between the two and forced Angelica forward, beating her soundly with no thought of preserving the fineness of her flesh. He was too far gone to notice the further changes in Semyon, but Angelica did, twisting her body to see, fighting with Sin.

The watchers were standing, applauding her fierceness. Half in her captor's arms, half out, shielding herself from the descending crop, she struggled and bit, her mask falling off when he grabbed at her hair.

Then . . . she held her breath as the first signs of the ruff appeared about Semyon's neck. Spreading over his shoulders, which rose higher. Down his back. His neck thickened and the iron collar was once again too small.

But he was stronger, far stronger than he'd been in the cellar. Blood pulsed in the veins, she could see it. She reached out a finger to feel the mighty pulse and his mind spoke to her.

Blood as blue as the sun that never sets. Do you remember our story, Angelica?

"Yes," she whispered.

The ice-wolves of long ago carried the Roemi upon their backs. And I shall carry you to freedom.

"Semyon!"

His hands reached to the iron collar around his neck and broke it apart. Then he took hold of hers, brushing away Sin's attempts to stop him.

Free, she still struggled to stand and she could not run away.

Man and wolf man were locked in battle upon the stage.

Chapter 18

Sin fought insanely hard, but Semyon soon overpowered him. The tall man writhed on the floor of the stage, his shoulders pinned by Semyon's huge front paws and his legs sprawled apart, also held down.

Semyon's eyes glowed with rage, his protective instincts fully awakened now. He lowered his shaggy head and clasped his jaws around Sin's throat.

His wheezing plea for mercy was drowned out by deafening applause from the excited crowd.

"Magnificent, Sin!"

"Best show yet!"

"More! Give us more!"

With horror dawning in her heart, Angelica saw the great fangs extend. One pressed into Sin's neck near the jugular vein. The man lay still, no longer fighting.

She kneeled, trying to separate them—and found that she was fighting Semyon. Controlled by instinct, his mind no longer what she would call human, he seemed seized by an ancient bloodlust.

She grabbed him by the ruff and he shook her off, but his jaws let go of the throat he so wanted to rip open.

Sin panted, getting his breath back but the pressure of the mighty paws holding him down would not permit him to move.

He muttered raw curses and Semyon's dripping jaws opened again.

Wider.

As if he was about to devour him, starting with the head.

The thought made Angelica's heart stop beating for several seconds. She could make no appeal to Semyon's conscience, for at the moment, he had none. He was, she thought wildly, no different than Sin now.

She looked into his eyes, tried to soothe him by stroking his huge head. Again he was unreachable. His consciousness was that of a wolf facing a fatal threat, on the lowest level, without the noble nature of his heroic ancestors among the Roemi. He had become an ice wolf, slavering and feral and utterly dangerous.

Still she reached out to him. The man she knew, wolf blood and all, was under the rippling fur. Her tentative touch to his breastbone caught him unawares and his stance shifted toward her, though he still held Sin down.

"Semyon, Semyon," she whispered desperately. "Do you not know me? Think . . . dear God . . . think and remember. You are more than a beast!"

The pointed oval pupils in his eyes expanded as he stared at her. He shook his shaggy head and they contracted again.

Had her plea been heard and understood? She had no way of knowing but she continued to stroke him, vowing to do it as long as he would let her.

She was only dimly aware of the grumbling audience, who seemed to have expected blood to flow—stage blood—in spectacular gouts.

Instead they saw a tableau of frozen terror without understanding how real it was and complained.

Semyon swung his head toward her again, as if he wanted to hear her voice. She murmured soothing words, encouragement to the man within the animal, words of love, tumbling over and over in an incoherent rush.

His ears twitched, listening.

Sin moaned beneath him and Semyon raised a long-nailed, heavy paw, about to crush it into the man's sweating face, but he stopped in midair and put it back on Sin's shoulder. Not quickly enough.

Sin had feral instincts of his own. The moment of inattention let him twist his prone body and knock the great wolf away, so that Semyon sat back on his haunches, then toppled.

Sin scrambled to his feet and made a dash for the door. Again the crowd screamed with delight, captivated by this new development. Semyon gathered his legs, poised to leap, but Angelica's cry made him botch it and he tumbled again, sprawling in an ugly way on the stage.

"The beast and the bitch!"

She went to him, desperately afraid that he was injured.

He gasped for breath, his sides heaving, and she saw that the change to human was beginning.

"He will become a man again." Sin's voice, quiet and sinister, came from the back of the darkness. "What am I bid?"

"Good show, Sin!" said the unseen man who had sounded so familiar. Angelica whirled and looked, looked, looked.

Who was he?

"I bid three thousand for the pair! For me and my wife!" he said triumphantly.

"Done." That was Sin's voice.

Huzzahs and shouts of approval split the air. And then there was silence. She heard footsteps.

Sin was coming back to the stage. But he was followed by—her heart sank as she recognized the couple—Mr. Congreve and Mrs. Congreve.

Angelica gasped. Had they recognized her face under the strapped mask?

Most likely not. Her hair had been pinned severely and her former master knew nothing of what she looked like naked.

Another question burned in her mind. Had they recognized Semyon? They had known him as a gentleman, dressed in civilized clothes, not a wolf man passing rapidly through the guises and changes of the night's obscene revelry.

He had been offered up as a sexual slave, naked, enchained. He had become a murderous beast. And a being in between those two, suspended between the real world of men and the supernatural realm of his kind.

She caught a whiff of the strong drink on their breath and noticed that they were swaying where they stood. They were drunk. No, most likely they were not aware that they had just purchased their honored guest and their former lady's maid.

There would be hell to pay when they did, she thought in panic.

Sin led them up into the light, and guided them to one side. He pulled Angelica up with a vicious yank, as Semyon stumbled to his feet and went to her, groggy again from the rapid shift in shape.

Sin stepped forward, acknowledging the applause of the enthusiastic crowd. They called to him in loud praise and shouted to the Congreves. The noise was deafening.

Angelica contrived to whisper to Semyon. "Stay with me.

We will find Antosha and go in their carriage, then we will escape."

She scarcely heard the rest, turned away from the Congreves to guide Semyon out first. But she did catch Sin's parting remark behind.

"Devil take them all," he said. To whom, she did not know. But he sounded resigned to letting them go. The overexcited guests might erupt in a riot if he did not, she thought.

They were moving through halls of a house that was nowhere near as grand as the Congreve mansion, and it was hard to struggle through.

The guests had begun to depart but still they chattered and many of them grabbed at Angelica and Semyon, pulling at hair and fondling their flesh if they could.

She whacked at the perpetrators, sometimes blindly, but they only laughed at her. Semyon growled when a woman's nails dug into the hot muscle of his chest and she squealed with delight.

The Congreves were just ahead, talking right and left to people they knew and people they didn't. She noted Mr. Congreve's hand upon his wife's arse, squeezing her roughly. The prize they had bid for and won had heightened the unhealthy sexual hunger that drove them both. To escape, she and Semyon and—oh, where was Antosha?

She looked around for Sin, but saw no sign of him. There—that was the door to the kitchen. If she could get free of the throng . . . she plucked a coat from a footman with an armful of them who was pushing through himself.

"Not yours, you filthy hussy," he said, leering at her and fighting her for it. Semyon pushed past her and took the man by the scruff of the neck, forcing him below the heads of the crowd, who noticed nothing of it.

In another second, the footman was unconscious and left

against a wall in a nook that opened off the hall. They had their pick and quickly threw on the heaviest and biggest garments. Angelica propped her foot on the marble base of a statue in the nook and broke off one crippling high heel of her sluttish boots, then did the same with the other. At least she was still shod and she could run.

She dashed back immediately, relieved to see that the Congreves were still blathering on to a gaggle of friends while they waited for their carriage to appear. As they had come late, it would be brought round first.

There were only seconds left in which to find Antosha. But Semyon was not where she had left him. He must have gone to the kitchen and that was where she found him, glimpsing the tweed coat that barely clothed his shoulders as he raced down the stairs to the cellar.

She hesitated at the top, standing guard. What if Lucy or the other two girls saw her there? But she saw no one but manservants who were unfamiliar to her, probably hired for the night. One or two cast admiring looks at her and she thought to look haughtily back, dismissing them with her cold, silent gaze.

If she had been called a bitch, she would be one.

Semyon came back up. "He is not there," he whispered to her. A manservant overheard.

"Is it that dirty fellow you are looking for? He is over there. Very sick, he is."

Semyon went to where the servant pointed, followed by Angelica. "We must hurry—oh, dear God!"

Antosha had been left on the floor, and he was barely breathing. His lips were blue and the hollows under his eyes deeply sunken. He was limp when Semyon kneeled to lift him, his hands flopping nervelessly.

Angelica looked about for some garment that would cover

him and settled for a tablecloth thrown in a wash basket, stained with wine.

Swiftly, ignored by the hurrying servants moving all around them, they contrived to wrap Antosha in it. Semyon eased him onto his shoulder. Between the white of the cloth and the red blotches it bore, the injured man inside it could well have been a corpse.

Angelica was not heartened by the feeble moan that came from him as they returned to the hall.

As the jostling crowd moved slowly outside, she found the Congreves again, hallooing to their driver and looking around for the couple they had bid for. They seemed too drunk to be capable of sexual play tonight, no matter how outré. But they would be sure to claim what they had paid for, Angelica thought, and demand their money's worth.

There were servants in the Congreve livery about the carriage and she stifled a cry when she recognized Jack among them.

He was not drunk and he would remember her. She looked to Semyon, who marched on, staying ahead of her. She saw Jack turn and his eyes widen as he caught the sight of Semyon bullying through the dispersing crowd.

Some unspoken communication flowed between the two men. Jack whispered to the men who rode on the back of the carriage when they stepped down. "They will help you with that, sir," he said to Semyon. With their unquestioning assistance, the injured man was lifted to the high, closed box where the driver sat and murmured words were exchanged. No one seemed to see. Mrs. Congreve was looking in the small silk bag that hung from her wrist, scrabbling in it like a rodent.

"My pills . . . I feel nauseous. Where are my pills?" she snapped at her husband.

"I did not take them, dearest," he said in a nasty tone.

Angelica kept looking for Sin. It seemed impossible that they would escape his clutches so easily. Then she saw him. He had an arm draped around Lucy's shoulders, as if they were fair and white and she a great beauty. She reached into her apron pocket and handed him a very small bottle.

Not whiskey, Angelica thought. A tincture of laudanum—the stuff came in such bottles. She was sure it was, even from this distance. He uncorked it and drank it down. No wonder his brain was so addled. Thank God for another bit of luck. But she turned away from the pair all the same.

Jack had gone to Mrs. Congreve, fawning and making such a fuss over her and helping her so clumsily that she slipped inside the carriage to avoid him.

He bowed to Mr. Congreve. "Did you enjoy your evening, sir?"

"Quite." Mr. Congreve belched as he was assisted in and Jack grimaced at the smell. "We drank ourselves half to death," he said to Jack. "Tell the driver to go slowly."

"I will, sir."

Congreve's thick hand extended out from the carriage and signaled to his footman. "Jack! Fetch rags at once! Mrs. Congreve has been sick all over the back! Blast! Never mind going slow! Get us home!"

Semyon and Angelica exchanged a look as Jack swung up on the running board and banged on the driver's box.

He gestured to them, and they understood his meaning. *Follow.*

They would have to do that on foot, for they had not a shilling between them. And they had only a vague idea of where they were, and that was gathered from the idle talk going around them. None of that mattered.

They turned to each other and spoke the same name at the same time.

"Antosha."

They had to hurry. They took to their heels and fled.

Chapter 19

"Which way?" she asked, breathless from trying to keep up with him.

"Just follow."

"How can you be so sure of how to go?" She clasped the open front of the coat around her, mindful of the scanty thing beneath. The heelless boots were difficult to run in and her feet rolled from side to side each time they touched the ground.

"Their scent trail lingers in the air, of course. It is how I found you." Semyon lifted his head and grabbed her hand, running down a different street, not one she would have picked. It was entirely deserted. But he seemed very sure of himself. "You have a distinctive smell about you."

"A carriage smells like a carriage," she replied.

"This one reeks of Mrs. Congreve's perfume and vomit," he replied shortly. He seemed completely restored to his former self in outward appearance and manner.

But having seen his savagery toward Sin not two hours

ago, Angelica was still uneasy. An argument, if there was one, at the Congreves' house, might trigger worse.

"Warm enough?" he asked, glancing at her.

"Of course not. You saw what I had on."

He nodded and slowed, whiffing the air again. This street too was deserted and he seemed momentarily at a loss. The moonlight showed the troubled look on his face and the scudding clouds across it were like the shadows on his own.

"Are we lost?"

"No. What happened there—I was thinking of it. It was like a nightmare that went on and on."

She nodded. "We cannot talk of it now. And I am sure there is much you do not remember."

"I nearly killed Sin," he said, turning to her. "Why did you stop me?"

"I—I don't know."

He shook his head, not seeming satisfied with that answer. "We need never speak of it. No one has to know."

"The Congreves might." She still thought she had not been recognized by them, but rescuing Antosha might be her undoing. She could not leave Semyon to do it alone.

"There is a way around everything," he said staunchly. Little by little he seemed to be becoming the man she'd known again. But the freakish celebration of lust—their cruel imprisonment—all that would haunt them.

It was madness to think on it. On they went.

Even knowing his wolf nature as she did, she was surprised when they came at last to the house they sought. She had last been here less than a month ago—it could have been a lifetime.

The tall windows blazed in the front.

"Mrs. Congreve must have roused the household," he said. "Where do they keep their carriage?"

"Around the back. They share a small house for it with another family, so you will see two."

He looked at the house again, then at her. "Where to look first?"

She cast a worried glance at the blazing windows. "Jack sees to her when Mr. Congreve is too drunk to do it. The other men see to the horses and putting the carriage away."

"Antosha was with the driver," Semyon said softly. "So let us look in the carriage house first. They have been here for some time and he may have been moved."

"Jack can be trusted," she said. "A word to him is often enough."

He nodded. "Lead the way."

She took him by the hand this time, noticing that he was moving his head in the air, hearing, smelling, seeing, in a way that was more wolf than human. But he said nothing.

The large painted wood doors were bolted shut, of course. Semyon went to the side of the freestanding house. "Is there a window?"

"In the back, yes."

They went that way and he kneeled, letting her climb on his back to open it and wriggle in.

She tiptoed past the horses in their stalls, who lifted their heads and whickered curiously at her, and went to the bolted doors, sliding the tongue of wood out and letting him in.

Side by side were two nearly identical carriages but he would have known even in the dark which one belonged to the Congreves. Its sides were streaked where Mrs. Congreve had puked out the window.

Angelica did not feel sorry for the woman in the least. She stepped up onto the running boards, and opened the small door to the enclosed driver's box—there was nothing there, no trace of the tablecloth they'd wrapped him in, not a bit of bandage from the arm she'd doctored for him. Semyon rose beside her, peering in.

"Can you tell anything?"

He gave her the faintest of smiles. "Only that he was alive when he was taken down from here."

"How do you know that?"

"A dead man smells very differently from a live one. No, Antosha was breathing and perhaps even struggling. I am picking up a trace of sweat."

She clambered down. That at least was good news.

"Where to now?" she asked him.

"The house."

She bolted the double doors from the inside and they both went out the window this time so no one would know they had intruded.

"The back door," she whispered. "Kittredge often steals out that way to visit his sweetheart and does not lock it."

He nodded, letting her lead him. They went up that set of stairs, which had an untended look, unlike the grand front that faced the street.

"What is that little house?" he whispered, pointing to a structure some yards from the house.

"The night closet, of course. For the servants, not the Congreves."

He looked at her as if he should have known that. "The Pack does not use them. Too vulnerable. We would hate to be caught with our breeches down and our furry arses up."

The absurd joke cheered her, especially since he seemed to be sure that Antosha was alive. They had escaped from a London hell and so were they.

But she could not quite laugh. "We may be caught if we are not careful."

"What, do you think the Congreves would go to the authorities and complain that the sex slaves they bought ran away? Or demand restitution from the infamous St. Sin?"

"Other people besides constables can be paid to find runaways."

He chucked her under the chin. "When they are sober, they will consider the whole experience a drunken escapade and consider themselves best shut of it."

"Perhaps." She still wondered whether either of them had been recognized. But that didn't matter at that moment. She focused her thoughts on the missing man and mentally walked through the house.

Where would Jack have hidden him?

She looked up to a window high under the eaves, not far from the one she had shared with another maidservant.

Jack's room showed a faint light, as if from a solitary candle. From where they were in the darkness she could see a wavering glimmer. She pointed. "Look, that is Jack's room and someone is there. But we cannot climb so high."

"Is there a way through the house that the servants use?"

"We would be noticed."

An anguished sound came from inside and Semyon looked at her. "Mrs. Congreve?"

She nodded. "Yes, I think so. Still sick, by the sound of it. The entire household comes to a stop when she demands attention."

His gaze held hers. "It is a poor chance, but it is all we have."

She hesitated. "But Jack would care for Antosha until we could spirit him away."

Semyon's expression was grave. "Angelica. What if he perished during the night? We cannot put your friend in such danger too."

She had to admit that he was right. "Then come with me,"

she said after a little while. "We can try—but these clothes underneath! If only we could disguise ourselves better—"

She thought of the laundry room and its boiler, and the racks of clothes left to dry there in the winter, waiting to be ironed and starched. Certainly it would not be in use at this hour.

"I have an idea," she said, brightening.

They went that way first. As she had thought, there were plenty of plain, serviceable clothes that would help them to pass for servants at first glance.

She took off the strapped corset and stuffed it into the banked embers under the boiler. Let it burn. She hated it. Then she donned a dark gown and apron, and concealed her hair beneath a wrinkled cap.

He borrowed the everyday clothes of the tallest footman and found shoes in a bin that the cook kept for tramps.

"We are the perfect couple," he said, when they had dressed hastily. "And now, let us get what we came for."

She went to the door between the laundry room and the kitchen and peered out, seeing nothing but the old cat asleep in its basket by the hearth.

Mrs. Congreve's wretched groans were audible even here, and she suspected she had guessed aright: most of the servants had been dragged from bed to dance attendance upon her.

They stole through the corridor that the servants used and up the back stairs to the rooms under the eaves.

She paused with him on the landing. The faint, flickering light she'd seen from below, outside, came from under the door of Jack's room. Angelica tiptoed to it and knocked softly, calling his name in a whisper.

She turned and motioned to Semyon to come on when Jack opened the door to her. On his bed lay the missing man, his eyes open, huge in the half-light, pathetically grateful to see her.

Semyon pushed past her and kneeled at his side. "Antosha," he said. "Forgive me."

"Why?" the man on the bed asked weakly.

"I had no thought for danger."

Antosha's mouth contorted in something like a smile. "You never have."

"I never dreamed that—"

Antosha raised a feeble hand and waved the rest of it away. "Never mind. I am not dead yet, as you can see. Bring me home."

Angelica dashed away her tears. He seemed like a ghost, still partly wrapped in the white cloth that looked far too much like a shroud.

"Yes, Antosha. On my back if I have to."

He leaned down and picked up the frail figure with Jack's assistance. Angelica said nothing as they went back the way they had come, miraculously unseen.

Bringing up the rear, she bumped into a new housemaid carrying a slop bowl and cursing Mrs. Congreve under her breath.

The girl did not give her a second look.

They trudged through silent streets, looking a good deal more respectable but feeling much colder since they had left the coats they'd taken in the laundry room. Angelica stuck close to Semyon's side, matching his long strides with difficulty, looking down now and then at Antosha, who murmured an occasional words of encouragement to both of them.

It was another hour before they turned in to the street that led to St. James's Square.

There was the house of the Pack. The windows showed

thin slices of light at the edges of the opaque blinds that covered them.

Semyon mounted the stairs as Antosha looked up. "Never thought I would see this house again," he murmured in a voice so faint that Angelica feared for him. "Thank you both. Thank you . . ." His voice trailed off.

She knocked as Semyon told her to do, in a particular rhythm that brought someone to the door in seconds.

Ivan opened it, struck dumb at the sight of the three. He ushered them in hastily, looking to the right and left of the street and seeing no one.

"We have had men out day and night looking for you all over London," he said, a look of profound concern in his eyes. There were tears there too. "Where—" One look at Antosha's hollow-eyed face and the housemaster said nothing more. "Bring him to a bedchamber. Someone will fetch a physician." Semyon walked that way. But Ivan's hand stopped Angelica from following.

Semyon didn't seem to notice and she bowed her head when Ivan pointed upstairs, obeying him humbly.

Chapter 20

Through the window, a bleary-eyed Sin observed an uncertain sun come up and hang in the sky, low clouds weighing it down. "Must you stand there?" Victor complained. "You look like a figure from a tomb."

Sin ignored the remark. "Did you sleep well?"

"Tolerably. I heard that it was quite a show."

Sin unclasped his hands from behind his back and moved to sit in an armchair by the bed that Victor was in.

The younger man threw off the covers. "One of the guests came up here. Quite drunk but very pretty. And extremely overstimulated by what she had seen."

"Ah," Sin said. "Did you offer her relief then?"

Victor grinned, swinging his legs out, still clad in small-clothes but barefoot.

"She came in that door, peeked around, and straddled me."

"How romantic."

Victor yawned again, rubbing at his hair and making it look worse. "She got what she wanted."

"And you?"

The younger man rose and walked to the chest of drawers, pouring water from an ewer into a large china bowl and bending over it to splash his face and neck. He reached for a crumpled towel and dried himself absentmindedly. "It kept me from thinking, so that was good." He tossed the towel on the floor. "What of our captives? Still alive?" He added. "The ones in the cellar, I mean."

Sin managed a thin smile. "Yes, they are alive. Your stepsister turned out to be a remarkable performer for a novice."

Victor gave a slight shudder. "And did she wear that corset you showed me?"

"What there was of it." Sin let his head loll back against the chair, looking utterly weary.

The other man nodded and slipped on breeches that did not seem to fit. The smallclothes bunched underneath and he spent a minute trying to get one to fit well with the other, unbuttoning and rebuttoning the breeches flap. "Damnation. These are not mine." He looked irritably around the room. "I wonder who else came in while I was sleeping."

"Whoever the man was, he has gone home in yours," Sin said.

Victor scowled. "I have another pair in a trunk somewhere. Can we not go back to the new house, Sin? Going from one place to the next has got me in a swivet."

"Poor you," Sin said indifferently.

"You might show some concern for me. We are still partners. I did lead you to my stepsister."

Sin extended his arms and clasped his hands, stretching them. "She is gone now."

"What?" Victor stopped. "Oh, right—I suppose she would be. But I thought you were going to sell her for just one night and take it from there."

"You mean break her down from there." He shook his head. "No, she took matters into her own hands."

"How?" Half-dressed, Victor sat down on the bed and felt under it with his foot for shoes.

"She turned into a wildcat," Sin said with grudging admiration. "I think the costume helped. But she was difficult to control, even chained to Semyon."

"Did you not drug him?"

"Of course. And I thought of drugging her. But I was glad I did not—she is spirited and the crowd loved to see her fight."

A shadow of something like guilt crossed the younger man's face. "I hope she was not injured."

Sin looked at him fiercely, drawing his lips back over his teeth. "Scratches. Stripes. That sort of thing. But Semyon nearly did me in."

Victor waved a hand dismissingly. "In shackles and chains? He is only a man, after all, no matter what you say."

"Ah, he is more than that. He showed himself as a beast last night."

"I suppose the crowd loved that too," Victor said. "I will watch next time. Him, anyway."

"There will not be a next time. He too has escaped. And the other one, the scrawny one. Angelica contrived to do it when she left with the couple who bought her."

"Good God! Is she—"

"The three of them are gone. There was the usual commotion when the carriages were brought round and I'm afraid I was rather drunk. I saw that she did not get in to the Congreves' carriage and that it drove off without her or Semyon."

"The Congreves? But that is where—she was Mrs. Congreve's lady's maid. Hinch took her from there, you know that."

Sin only shrugged. "They were about to sack her or so the old man bragged at his club."

"You hear everything."

Sin smiled slightly. "I try to."

"So you sold them a girl they owned. Such cheek!"

"They didn't own her and I don't think they recognized her. But they were willing to pay three thousand pounds for her and Semyon together. Special offer at couples' rate," he said mockingly.

"You don't mean that."

"Married people pay handsomely. When they pay." He reached into a waistcoat pocket. "A note came from Mr. Congreve as I was mounting the stairs to say good morning to you."

He handed over a folded piece of paper, which Victor read in silence.

Sin—

Goods not delivered. Offer canceled. An entertaining show, though. Much obliged.

Yours in haste, and very truly etc.

Jasper Congreve

Victor looked up as he refolded the note and handed it back to his partner. "Did we even recoup the cost of the party, Sin?"

The older man scowled. "Do you think I sit down with a ledger and tot up figures the second the sun comes up the next day?"

"Forgive me," Victor said acidly. "I sometimes forget that a great impresario cannot be bothered with such trifles."

"See to it yourself." St. Sin seemed bored. "I hired fifteen men servants, and Lucy demanded two additional maids. A cold collation, delivered on trays. Bread. Ale. Ice. The cost of the wine was astronomical, but one cannot water it. Guests must be good and drunk before they part with their money, even rich guests."

"It is a shame that Congreve reneged."

Sin pulled up his sleeve and showed the scratches on his arm. "She might have done this to him. He would be no less angry."

"I suspect old Congreve would have enjoyed it. And his dear wife too."

"Dear me. You will soon be as decadent as I am," Sin said dryly. "If we break even, that is that. But I had wanted to open a more permanent establishment."

Victor raised a quizzical eyebrow. "Are you sure? Illicit parties with no fixed address are all the rage—half the fun is finding them," he said.

Sin shook his head. "I am too old for such fashionable nonsense. But vice is a good business, although it is beginning to tell on me. I have an agonizing headache."

"I will ask Lucy to mix you a powder."

Sin pressed his fingertips to his temples. "Tell her to make it a strong one. I feel as if someone is inside my head and trying to talk to me."

"Is it the voice of reason?" Victor joked. "Try to listen to it."

"Shut up," Sin growled. He lifted himself out of the armchair and went to his own chamber to sleep it off.

Semyon and Angelica lay together in a troubled sleep. He awoke with a start and drew her close.

"Is it the sun?" she asked sleepily. "Draw the blinds."

"No, dearest." He kissed her forehead, then her lips. Her exhausted eyes did not open. "But I will close them so you can sleep."

He got up, and she did look as he went to the window, her

troubled mind eased by his animal physicality and glorious nakedness.

Fully male. Entirely human.

The sight of him was reassuring, but it did not completely erase the fear at the edge of her overwhelming drowsiness. She welcomed him with loving murmurs when he returned, pulling the covers up over his brawny shoulders and then nestling against the fine dark fur on his chest.

They had simply stripped and tumbled in to bed when he had come up, telling her briefly that a physician had come for Antosha, who was resting comfortably. She had not wanted to ask what was to be done about her.

She looked up at him, a little more awake, worried about him. "Was it a bad dream then?"

He smiled sadly. "Yes. We are both going to have those for some time to come."

"Tell me of yours," she whispered.

"Ah, Angelica," he said, "I was lucky to have remembered so little of it. But it stayed in my mind, it seems. In sleep I see—"

"What?"

"St. Sin. As if he were a devil but he is dressed as a gentleman. I am fighting with him."

"You did."

"Sometimes he is winning and sometimes I am." He sighed wrenchingly. "I am no more than a savage beast in his eyes. But I know that I am. Do you understand?"

She nodded. Every agonizing minute of it came back to her as he spoke. She squeezed her eyes shut and tears rolled down. Angelica brushed them away before they touched his skin but he knew she was crying.

"In the dream that woke me, I was about to tear out his throat. But you stopped me."

She clasped him more tightly, willing the memories away.

He dropped a kiss on her tousled hair. "I had thought of myself as a civilized man, you know. The picture of an English gentleman. But what lies underneath is savage indeed."

"Speak no more of it," she begged him. "Try to sleep."

He hugged her in arms that were as comforting as they were strong. "Yes, you are right. The aftermath of this will not be pretty, but it is time someone put a stop to Sin."

"Yes," she whispered.

"Ivan told me that our contacts at court know of this—we dared not wait to tell them, in case he left the country. They will do a thorough investigation—ah, me. You must not know of this. My dearest, I will take you away, to the country. We will both go as soon as I—"

"Shhh," she said.

"My dear, forgive me. You need to sleep."

"And so do you."

Warm in each other's embrace, claimed by exhaustion that swallowed them, they drifted off again, each dreaming of nameless horrors—what they had endured and seen and what they only imagined.

Semyon, tossing, spoke to his tormentor in his nightmare.

You are the one who is not human, Sin. There is no mercy in you.

Fully wolf, he stared at the tall man on stage, hearing the crowd laugh and scream at them both.

"And you are a dying dog on a chain," Sin replied. His crop slashed and cracked, maddening Semyon.

But in his dream, he did not leap at the man or tear his throat.

He fixed Sin with a piercing gaze that held him perfectly still in the spotlight. So piercing that Semyon could enter the other man's mind.

No mercy. No kindness. No soul. He pressed deep into Sin's disordered brain without touching him.

"Ahh!" A single, excruciating scream came from Sin's mouth.

You are empty. Empty.

In Semyon's nightmare, the final word echoed once and shattered through the inchoate fog in his own mind. Again he awoke, gasping, feeling cold all over.

Angelica slept. He would not tell her of this. He settled down beside her, brooding, his body taut with nameless fear.

Across town, in Sin's chamber, there was a real scream, but those that heard it were elsewhere in the house and did nothing.

The scream came from Sin. He fell back rigidly upon his soiled pillow, his mouth contorted and his eyes rolling wildly as his body jerked.

He saw only the eyes of a wolf in front of him. Golden eyes that pierced him through and through.

Then he died.

Chapter 21

Months later . . .

"Shall we let the cubs out, Natalya? Or do they want to come in?"

The yips on the side of the door that led to an enclosed entryway had grown louder.

The other woman laughed, running a comb through her endless hair. "Hard to tell. But not, in, please. Not until I have finished my braids and put them up. They bite at the ends and there are so many of them."

Angelica nodded. "Ten is a large litter, though it did not seem so when they were tiny and slept so much. Poor Sabatchka. They all want to nurse at once and their milk teeth are in."

Natalya began the first braid, plaiting the strands of glossy hair in a peaceful rhythm. "Little beasts. I suppose I should make them scraped meat in broth and see how they like that."

Angelica dusted the flour from her hands. Her apron, she decided, was a lost cause. "You will spoil them."

"Children and puppies need a bit of spoiling now and

then," Natalya replied. She finished the braid and threw it over her shoulder, beginning on the next as she stared thoughtfully at the bread dough set in bowls in the sunniest spot in the kitchen. "That should rise well—ow!"

Semyon had come in from another room inside the house and not the entryway. He tugged the tail of the finished braid. "What about men? Don't we need spoiling?"

"Men are born spoiled," Natalya retorted. "Your mothers begin it and the women who love you keep right on with it."

"An excellent plan," he murmured, then spoke to his wife. "And what are you doing?"

She waved a hand at the smooth lumps of dough. "What does it look like?"

"Making molehills out of mountains, I would say."

Angelica laughed and flicked her apron at him, dusting him with a small cloud of flour from it. "Come back in the afternoon when it has baked and you can have some with jam and butter."

"I will stay right here," he said, "and guard the jam or there will be none. The last jar disappeared mysteriously and it was Natalya's best."

"Second best," she mocked him. She had come to the end of the second braid and that too was flipped over a shoulder. "I hide the best for Ivan."

"Then he is a lucky man," Semyon said.

"Tell him that," Natalya said, rising to go to the mirror and pin her braids into the crown.

"Ah, your hair is beautiful that way," Angelica said. "I must try that style." She went to stand behind Natalya, who placed the last of the pins and moved away, laughing.

Semyon came up behind Angelica once she was alone and nuzzled her ear, peeking at the looking glass to see if she liked it. She was smiling. "That tickles."

"So long as it gives you pleasure, my dear wife."

"Mmm. It does." His arms had encircled her waist and she rested her arms over them.

"Are you happy in Heraldshire?"

"Yes. But you promised to tell me why we came here in such a rush and you never did."

"Then I have been remiss," he said into her neck, making the "s" vibrate against her skin, which made her smile again.

"It has been two weeks, Semyon. The fresh air is lovely but—"

"But what?" He straightened and stopped his teasing.

"I will miss London in the autumn. It is when the theater season starts and the balls begin again and there are new pictures at the academies for the art critics to quarrel over—"

"The city holds many pleasures. We shall return, my dear." His voice was calm and he seemed to be taking her seriously. "After what happened, though, it seemed best to spend the summer here."

"I understand. So long as we can go back." That was what had been on her mind, and he had not been up often enough for her to ask the question.

"Of course."

"Have you seen Antosha?"

"Not yet."

"He is happier here, I think," Angelica said. "His injury still troubles him and he likes to just sit in the sun. I expect it is good for him."

"You are thoughtful to think so, Angelica. It was he who recommended Heraldshire in the first place."

"I did not know that."

Semyon nodded, putting his face next to hers so that their reflection in the looking glass seemed to be a double portrait. "He said that it was flat, which made it ideal for walking, and had no forests, so that the views went on forever. And there was the healthful sea breeze and so on and so forth."

"The local folk seem rather wary of us."

He only laughed. "Well, not you. More Natalya, I should think. She went out in all weathers to walk with Sabatchka and sing Russian songs and made herself the talk of the tavern for a while. They have never seen a dog that is so white and so fluffy, I heard."

"And so big with all those puppies heaving inside her," Angelica reminded him.

"They are farm folk and puppies are nothing new to them. I think it is her bright clothes and her braids that made people wonder."

Angelica turned in his arms. "Natalya has made friends, even if some think her odd."

"She is a charming girl."

She whispered into his ear.

"No? Really?" Semyon said with delight. "Good old Ivan. He will be thrilled to hear—"

"He must only hear it from her," Angelica said sternly.

"Yes, of course. I will keep my mouth shut. But it is happy news. So that is why you two are suddenly so domestic."

She took his hand and led him away from the mirror into the sitting room. "There is nothing else to do."

"Really? I can think of something." He moved closer to her on the settee. And closer. And closer. Until she was squeezed against the armrest and his thigh.

"Semyon, whatever is on your mind?"

He put his lips to her ear again. "Your succulent thighs. Your rosy breasts and unbelievably long nipples. Your hair, like dark fire. How I long to see it tumbled over a pillow and you under me as I—"

"Yes, well" —a high color came and went in her cheeks— "I thank you for that shower of compliments but we do need to talk, my dearest."

His face fell and he leaned back into the settee cushions.

"Oh. Those are words that put fear into the hearts of the strongest men."

"But we do need to."

He sat straight, not sure from her tone if she was joking or not. "What is the matter?"

She paused, collecting herself while she plucked at a loose thread in the material of the settee. "I—I am with child, Semyon."

"No!"

She would not look at him. "Yes," she said in a diffident voice.

"How did that happen?" he asked solemnly.

"In the usual way—" She looked up and saw him grinning at her, then grabbed a pillow and flung it at him. "Oh, you are a bad man to tease me so!"

"But you like me that way." He was laughing, protecting himself with the pillow he'd caught from her immediate assault with another one.

She was laughing, breathless, when she stopped hitting him. "I love you, Semyon. Does my news make you happy?"

He tossed both pillows to the floor and replaced them with the wife he adored, taking her into his arms and kissing her with all the tenderness his heart possessed.

"More than you will ever know," he said softly when he let her take a breath. "Much more. I shall love you forever. You are an angel indeed."

And then they lay down together . . .

Check out Sylvia Day's PRIDE AND PASSION,
coming soon from Brava . . .

"What type of individual would you consider ideal to play this role of suitor, protector, investigator?" Jasper asked finally.

Eliza's head tilted slightly as she pondered her answer. "He should be quiet, even-tempered, and a proficient dancer."

"How do dullness and the ability to dance signify in catching a possible murderer?" he queried, scowling.

"I did not say 'dull,' Mr. Bond. Kindly do not put words into my mouth. In order to be seen as a true threat for my attentions, he should be someone that everyone would believe I would be attracted to."

"You are not attracted to handsome men?"

"Mr. Bond, I dislike being rude. However, you leave me no choice. The point of fact is that you clearly are not marriage material."

"I am quite relieved to hear a female recognize that," he drawled.

"How could anyone doubt it?" She made a sweeping gesture with her hand. "I can more easily picture you in a swordfight or fisticuffs than I can see you enjoying an afternoon of croquet or after dinner chess. I am an intellectual, sir. And while I do not mean to say that you are lacking in mental acuity, you are obviously built for more physically strenuous pursuits."

"I see."

"Why, anyone would take one look at you and ascertain that you are not like the others at all! It would be evident straightaway that I would never consider a man such as you with even remote seriousness. Quite frankly, sir, you are not my type of male."

A slow smile began in his dark eyes, then moved downward to curve his lips. It was arresting. Slightly wicked. Troublesome.

Eliza did not like trouble overmuch.

He glanced at the earl. "Please forgive me, my lord, but I must speak bluntly in regards to this subject. Most especially because this is a matter of life and death."

"Quite right," Melville agreed. "Straight to the point, I always say. Time is too precious to waste on inanities."

"Agreed." Jasper glanced back at Eliza, his mischievous smile widening. "Miss Martin, forgive me, but I must point out that your inexperience is limiting your understanding of the situation."

"Inexperience with what?"

"Men. More precisely, fortune hunting men."

"I would have you know," she retorted, bristling, "that in my six years on the marriage market I have had more than enough experience with gentlemen in want of funds."

"Then why," he drawled, "do you not know that they are successful for reasons far removed from social suitability?"

Eliza blinked. "I beg your pardon?"

"Women do not marry fortune hunters because they can

dance and sit quietly. They marry them for their appearance
and physical prowess—two attributes you have already estab-
lished that I have."

"I do not see—"

"Clearly, you do not, so I shall explain." His smile continued to grow. "Fortune hunters who flourish do not strive to
satisfy a woman's intellectual needs. Those can be met through
friends and acquaintances. They do not seek to provide the type
of companionship one enjoys in social settings or with a game
table between them. Again, there are others who can do so."

"Mr. Bond—"

"No, they strive to satisfy in the only position that is theirs
alone, a position that some men make no effort to excel in. So
rare is the skill, that many a woman will disregard other con-
siderations in favor of it."

She growled softly. "Will you get to the point, please?"

"Fornication," his lordship said, before returning to mumbling to himself.

Eliza shot to her feet. "I beg your pardon?"

As courtesy dictated, both her uncle and Jasper rose along
with her.

"I prefer to call it 'seduction,'" Jasper said, his eyes laughing.

"I call it ridiculous," she rejoined, hands on her hips. "In
the grand scheme of life, do you collect how little time a person spends abed when compared to other activities?"

His gaze dropped to her hips. The smile became a full-
blown grin. "That truly depends on who else is occupying
said bed."

"Dear heavens." Eliza shivered at the look Jasper was giving her now. It was certainly *not* a bug-under-the-glass look.
No, it was more triumphant. Challenged. Anticipatory. For
some unknown, godforsaken reason she had managed to prod

the man's damnable masculine pride into action. "While I acknowledge that a man's brain might traverse such channels of thought, I cannot see a woman's doing so."

"But is it not men whom you wish to affect with this scheme?"

She bit her lower lip. Clever, clever man. He knew quite well that she had no idea how men's minds worked. She had no notion of whether he was correct, or simply tenacious about securing work.

"Give me a sennight," he offered. "One week to prove both my point and competency. If at the end you do not agree with one or the other, I will accept no payment for services rendered."

And don't miss Brava's Christmas anthology,
KISSING SANTA CLAUS,
featuring Donna Kauffman, Jill Shalvis, and
HelenKay Dimon, coming next month.

Turn the page for a preview from
Donna's story, "Lock, Stock, and Jingle Bells."

"It's been a long day, there's a lot to do." Holly lifted the bag. "Thank you for this, it was very thoughtful."

"If there's anything else I can do to help—"

"You've already gone above and beyond the call of duty here."

"Like I said, it's what I do, and I saw the light on." Sean tried a smile. "I also make a good listener. Family my size, you learn early. It can't be easy, leaving England, coming back to your hometown, taking over the business."

She held the bag a little closer to her chest, like a shield, but didn't say anything.

"If it helps, I know a little something about that."

She dipped her chin, and he found himself reaching out to tip it back up again. "Hey, I didn't say that to make you feel bad. But I do know about having plans derailed and a life you never thought you'd end up with being dumped in your lap."

She stared into his eyes and for the first time he felt he was really looking at Holly Bennett.

"You probably think I'm being a bit of a spoiled brat," she

said. "I mean, you came home because of an unspeakable tragedy, while my parents just retired. Which, at their age—"

"Yes, but most parents don't retire and head off to a new life and dump their old life on their only child."

She tilted her head slightly. "I thought you and my parents were friends."

"We are. I love your folks. But that doesn't mean I automatically vouch for all their decisions."

"Did you regret coming back to run your family restaurant? You seem—"

"Happy? I am. Very. And I didn't necessarily expect to be. Turned out that all my training has benefited me just as much, if not more, in taking over Gallagher's as it would have if I'd gone off on my own in DC like I planned. But I was lucky. I was already heading in a direction very similar to my folks, and their folks before them. It was more a detour down the same path, than a whole new journey."

"If you had come back and hadn't been happy . . . would you have stayed anyway?"

"I don't know. I have the benefit of coming from a very large family. So, it's possible I'd have trained one of them, or a handful of them, to take over, and I'd have gone back to my original plan of opening a more upscale establishment. They'd have only been a few hours apart, so it's possible I could have run one, and overseen the management of the other."

"Why didn't you go ahead and do that anyway? Have your cake, and all that?"

He smiled easily. "Because I am happy here. I learned why it was that generations of Gallagher's have cooked and run restaurants, here and in Ireland. It suits me . . . perhaps more than that other world ever would have. And I still have the training. It's affected the menu here and there. I get to play a little with things that interest me. So I think I am having my cake."

She nodded, then fell silent again, apparently lost in thought.

"You know," he said, at length, "you didn't follow in your parents' footsteps, in terms of being a shopkeeper, or even in the antiques business, right? Your mom said you are an artist."

"I'm in advertising."

Sean knew that, but he also knew that, according to her mom, anyway, it was just what paid the bills. Art was her passion. "No one is going to fault you if you decide this isn't for you. Your mom—"

"Says she'd be fine with whatever my decision is."

"Well, then . . . ?"

Holly sighed lightly. "That's what she says. But it's not how I feel. Now that I'm here. I know what this meant to her. If she was truly okay with dismantling it, she'd have done so."

"There's a difference between being okay with it no longer being here . . . and quite another to be the one in charge of taking a beloved possession apart, piece by piece. Maybe she simply didn't have it in her, and knew that you being not so emotionally attached, might find that easier. I'm not trying to overstep here, but . . . it's your legacy to do with as you please, right? Maybe you should just think of it that way. It could be something you find you enjoy . . . or the sale of it could provide you with the nest egg to pursue your own dreams. Don't you think your parents would be happy with either outcome?"

She held his gaze for the longest time. "What I think is that I wish I could have this conversation as easily with them as I'm having it with you."

He smiled. "I know they're your parents, and nobody knows them better than you do. But if you want an outside friend's opinion—"

"I think I already have it." She smiled then. "And it's appreciated. More than you know."

"Anytime."

Time spun out and neither of them moved. Or stoppped smiling.

Maybe it was the late hour, maybe it was the sense of intimacy created by standing in the darkened shop, or the connection he felt they shared, lives being abruptly changed, or simply a childhood of separate, but shared memories of growing up in the same town, surrounded by the same things, the same people. Whatever it was, he found himself shifting a step closer. She didn't move away. And all he could think as he slowly dipped his head toward hers, was why had it taken half of his life to finally work up the nerve to kiss Holly Bennett.